CONTENTS

Chapter 1	1
Chapter 2	19
Chapter 3	43
Chapter 4	61
Chapter 5	75
Chapter 6	90
Chapter 7	109
Chapter 8	122
Chapter 9	134
Chapter 10	147
Chapter 11	162
Chapter 12	173
Chapter 13	185

CHAPTER 1

The meadow stretched before us like a postcard memory, rolling hills dotted with wildflowers swaying in the late afternoon breeze. Three weeks had passed since our first romantic picnic here, and I'd spent the intervening days looking forward to returning to the peaceful spot where Emmet and I had finally found some normalcy after the supernatural chaos at Nellie's Diner.

"I keep thinking about that chocolate cake your aunt made," Emmet said, adjusting the wicker basket Aunt Hecate had pressed into our hands with explicit instructions to "go somewhere beautiful and remember what happiness feels like." His fingers drummed against the steering wheel in the rhythm that meant he was genuinely relaxed. "Does she take requests?"

"Only if you're prepared to owe her a favor," I replied, watching familiar landmarks slide past the passenger window. The old cemetery, the abandoned gas station where Deputy Chen had found those strange symbols, the turnoff toward the diner. "Aunt Hecate doesn't do anything without expecting something in return. It's not malicious, just practical magic."

"I'm still getting used to the idea that magic has economics," Emmet admitted as we approached the final hill before our destination. "Supply and demand for supernatural services."

"Everything has a price. The trick is making sure you can afford what you're buying." I settled deeper into the passenger seat, anticipating the vista that would open before us as we crested the rise. "Though I have to admit, sometimes the cost surprises even me."

My voice died as the meadow revealed itself. Where three weeks ago we'd counted maybe half a dozen RVs scattered across the landscape like gentle giants at rest, now dozens of vehicles filled the space like a temporary city. Converted vans painted in bright colors clustered near the creek. Massive Class-A motorhomes sprouted satellite dishes and awnings that created outdoor rooms. Small travel trailers gathered around improvised fire pits while solar panels caught the late afternoon sun, transforming it into power for laptops, phones, and the thousand small devices that kept modern nomads connected to the world they'd temporarily left behind.

"Well," Emmet said, pulling over to absorb the transformation. "This is completely different. Looks like we weren't the only ones who thought this was the perfect spot."

I extended my witch senses carefully, scanning the area with the thoroughness that had become automatic since accepting my role as Bone Gap's supernatural consultant. The meadow's energy signature had changed dramatically. Where before I'd sensed peaceful stillness broken only by natural rhythms, now complex layers of human emotion created a symphony of feelings: contentment, frustration, excitement, homesickness, community pride, and underlying tensions that suggested not everyone was entirely happy with their neighbors.

But underneath the human complexity, the land itself remained fundamentally clean. No supernatural threats lurked beneath the surface. No ancient bindings waited to cause trouble. No entities fed on the gathered emotions or prepared elaborate supernatural traps. Just people being people in all their complicated, messy, beautiful glory.

"It's safe," I announced, then caught myself repeating the same words I'd used during our first visit. "Sorry, I know you didn't ask, but after everything we've been through..."

"But it's good to know," Emmet finished, echoing his response from three weeks ago. His smile carried the warmth of shared understanding. "I'm still getting used to thinking about whether places are safe in supernatural terms. Six months ago, my biggest worry was whether someone was carrying concealed weapons. Now I wonder if the local diner might be feeding people to supernatural entities."

"Welcome to my world," I said, unbuckling my seatbelt. "Though I have to say, this feels refreshingly normal. Complicated, but normal."

We climbed out of the car and walked into what felt more like a small town than temporary camping. The vehicles had arranged themselves into informal neighborhoods that reflected different approaches to nomadic living. Expensive motorhomes with their own landscaping occupied prime real estate near the creek, their owners having invested in comfort and convenience.

Converted school buses and cargo vans formed a more bohemian section toward the hills, painted with murals and sporting creative solutions to the challenges of tiny living. Family setups with kids' bikes and colorful camping chairs created suburban pockets of organization, complete with outdoor rugs and portable playsets.

"Afternoon!" called a voice from our left, and I turned to see a weathered man with a silver ponytail emerging from behind a well-maintained Airstream trailer. He wore the kind of hiking clothes that had seen serious use without losing their functionality, and his deeply tanned face carried the relaxed confidence of someone completely comfortable in his own skin. Lines around his eyes spoke of years spent squinting into distance and weather, but his smile was genuinely welcoming. "You folks looking for a spot to set up? I'm River Martinez."

A petite woman joined him before I could respond, her movements quick and energetic despite the obvious decades of experience written in her weathered hands and silver hair. Short gray curls framed a face that radiated warmth, and her flowing purple dress moved like water as she gestured. Silver jewelry caught the light as she extended her hand, and her grip was surprisingly firm. "I'm Willow. River and I have been doing this for five years, so folks tend to come to us with questions or problems."

"Sage and Emmet," I said, shaking hands that felt grounded and real in a way that immediately put me at ease. "We're from Bone Gap, just wanted to visit this beautiful spot again."

"Oh, you were here before the boom!" Willow laughed, gesturing at the expanded community around us with obvious pride and barely concealed concern. "Word got out on social media about this perfect free camping spot. Started with a few posts, then some YouTuber featured it, and now we've got a waiting list and everything."

River nodded, but I caught a note of careful

diplomacy in his expression. "It's been an adjustment. Most folks are great. We've got retirees taking the road trip they spent decades working to afford, digital nomads following their dreams, families homeschooling on the road and giving their kids experiences money can't buy. Real salt-of-the-earth travelers who understand that community makes this lifestyle work."

"Most folks?" Emmet asked, his law enforcement instincts picking up the same careful phrasing I'd noticed.

"Well," Willow said, choosing her words with the care of someone who'd learned that diplomacy prevented bigger problems, "some people approach van life differently than others. We try to maintain community harmony, but everyone has their own idea of what that means."

Her explanation was interrupted by loud voices carrying across the meadow, punctuated by the distinctive whine of professional camera equipment being adjusted and the sharp commands of someone accustomed to directing others.

Near the prominent oak tree that marked the meadow's most scenic camping spot, bright LED lights created an artificial sunrise despite the late afternoon hour, their harsh glare washing out the natural beauty of the golden light filtering through leaves.

"I need the lighting to hit at exactly this angle for authentic morning vibes," called a voice that carried the projection training of someone used to performing for audiences. "Can everyone else please keep the noise down? This is a professional shoot, and background noise ruins the audio quality."

The person directing the chaos had an androgynous, carefully disheveled appearance that somehow managed to look both outdoorsy and expensive. Their lightweight hiking gear bore designer labels, their artfully messy hair appeared professionally styled to suggest windswept adventure, and their natural charisma projected even at a distance. Everything about them screamed careful curation, from their perfectly weathered boots to their collection of expensive outdoor gear arranged for maximum visual impact.

But the elaborate camera setup told a different story. Professional-grade equipment worth thousands of dollars filled the space around the oak tree. Ring lights, reflectors, and stabilizing rigs created a mobile studio that had nothing to do with casual documentation and everything to do with content creation as serious business.

"That would be Dakota Rivers," River said quietly, his voice carrying the careful neutrality of someone who'd had this conversation before.

"Popular van life YouTuber. Twenty-five thousand subscribers and growing."

"Started showing up about a week ago," Willow added, her diplomatic tone layering subtle criticism beneath surface politeness. "Very dedicated to their craft."

I could see immediately why the community was struggling with Dakota's presence. Their expensive van setup dominated the best camping spot in the meadow, a location that offered the most scenic views and the easiest access to water. Their filming equipment monopolized shared spaces that other people wanted to enjoy for their own recreation and relaxation. Their demands for quiet during shoots disrupted the natural rhythm of camp life, turning neighbors into unwilling extras in someone else's performance.

"Some of us came here for peace and quiet," muttered a voice nearby, and I turned to see a man with unmistakable military bearing keeping his distance from Dakota's production. He had the broad shoulders and alert posture of someone who'd served in combat, but his weathered face carried the exhaustion of someone fighting invisible battles that followed him everywhere. His clothes were clean but worn, his van setup minimal and efficient, and his eyes held the hypervigilant quality of someone who'd learned that safety required constant attention. "Not to be background actors in someone's Instagram fantasy."

"That's Tank Williams," Willow said softly, her voice full of compassion. "Thomas, but everyone calls him Tank. Army veteran using van life for PTSD recovery. Good man, just needs his space and quiet to heal."

"And he's not getting either," Emmet observed, watching Dakota direct their filming crew to reposition equipment for the third time in as many minutes. The crew appeared to be other van lifers recruited as unpaid assistants, their body language suggesting this wasn't entirely voluntary participation.

Tank's jaw tightened as Dakota's voice rose again, demanding that someone move their camp chair because it was "creating visual clutter in the authentic nature setting." His hands clenched and unclenched at his sides, and I recognized the signs of someone fighting to maintain control over responses trained by military experience but inappropriate for civilian situations.

River noticed the same thing I did. He approached Dakota with diplomatic skill, his voice calm and reasonable. "Hey there, we usually try to keep filming equipment minimal during community hours when people are trying to relax and connect. Maybe we can work out a schedule that works for everyone?"

Dakota barely looked up from their camera

settings, their attention focused on technical details rather than the human beings around them. "This will just take a few more hours. My content helps promote van life and brings attention to amazing spots like this." They gestured expansively at the meadow with the confidence of someone who believed their own publicity. "I'm doing everyone a favor by showcasing this hidden gem to my followers. The exposure benefits the whole community."

The irony struck me immediately. Dakota's promotion of the "hidden gem" had apparently contributed to the meadow's transformation from peaceful retreat to crowded campground, creating the very problem they now seemed oblivious to causing.

"It's just that some folks come here to disconnect from exactly the kind of digital world your content represents," River persisted. "The constant filming can interfere with that healing experience."

"Then they shouldn't have chosen a lifestyle that's inherently social media worthy," Dakota replied with casual dismissiveness that made several nearby campers visibly flinch. "Van life is about freedom and authenticity and sharing those experiences with others. If they can't handle that being documented, maybe they should stick to traditional camping in designated campgrounds where they can hide from the modern world."

The response revealed everything I needed to know about Dakota's worldview. They saw the van life community not as neighbors to respect but as content opportunities to exploit. The people around them existed to provide authentic background for their carefully crafted narrative of nomadic freedom.

Willow and River exchanged a look that spoke volumes about previous conversations on this topic. Around the meadow, I noticed other van lifers pausing their evening routines to listen, their body language suggesting this wasn't the first such discussion and their patience was wearing thin.

I began analyzing the social dynamics with the same thoroughness I'd use for a potential supernatural threat. The skills translated surprisingly well. Dakota's charismatic on-camera persona clearly differed from their entitled off-camera behavior. They seemed to view the van life community as a film set rather than a neighborhood, treating shared spaces as their personal studio and fellow campers as unpaid actors in their ongoing performance.

"This feels like a powder keg," I murmured to Emmet as we continued walking through the meadow, observing the careful distance most people maintained from Dakota's elaborate setup. "All it needs is the right spark."

"I was thinking the same thing," he replied, his law enforcement experience reading the situation through a different lens but reaching identical conclusions.

Despite Dakota's disruptive presence, I found myself genuinely charmed by the rest of the van life community. River and Willow led us through their temporary neighborhood with obvious pride, explaining customs that had evolved organically over weeks of shared living. The morning coffee hour happened around their setup, where a large percolator provided caffeine for anyone who contributed beans or conversation. Evening community fires offered space for storytelling, music, and the kind of casual connection that formed the backbone of nomadic society. Informal skill-sharing sessions turned parking areas into classrooms where people taught everything from solar panel maintenance to bread baking in Dutch ovens.

"That's Maria over there," Willow pointed to a woman in her sixties teaching a small group about water conservation techniques. "Retired engineer who's traveled to forty-three states and counting. She knows more about RV systems than most mechanics."

A message board mounted on the side of River's van served as the community's central nervous system, covered with handwritten notes, printed schedules, and colorful announcements. Lost item notices promised rewards for missing camp chairs and phone chargers. Offers to share resources connected people with surplus supplies to those running low on essentials. Ride-sharing arrangements coordinated trips to town for groceries, laundry, and the thousand errands that kept nomadic life functional.

"It's like a small town," I told Willow as she showed us the informal library housed in weatherproof boxes mounted between two vans, books available for borrowing on the honor system. "But everyone chose to be here."

"That's exactly right," she said, her face lighting up with the enthusiasm of someone describing a dream made real. "No one's stuck with neighbors they can't stand or community rules they had no voice in creating. If the dynamic doesn't work, people can just load up and drive away. It creates a different kind of accountability because cooperation is genuinely voluntary."

The cooperation impressed me despite Dakota's obvious disruption. Children rode bikes between campsites while parents called gentle reminders about staying visible and respecting other people's spaces. Teenagers clustered around someone's van where a guitar provided soundtrack to conversations about dreams and destinations. Young adults worked on laptops, taking advantage of cellular hotspots and the last good light of day.

Retirees sat in folding chairs, sharing stories and advice accumulated over decades of experience.

As evening approached, people began emerging from their various setups with the comfortable ritual of neighbors gathering for shared time. Camp chairs materialized from storage compartments, coolers produced drinks both alcoholic and otherwise, and the central fire ring became a focal point for community life. Kids brought games and instruments, adults brought conversation and laughter, and the whole meadow settled into the peaceful rhythm of people choosing to spend time together.

The scene should have been perfectly peaceful, but Dakota was already setting up filming equipment around the fire ring, apparently planning to document the evening's community gathering without asking permission from anyone who might appear in the footage.

"The fire circle is kind of our sacred time," River suggested as Dakota adjusted camera angles and tested lighting equipment. "We usually keep devices put away so people can really connect with each other instead of performing for audiences."

"My followers love authentic community content," Dakota replied without looking up from their equipment, their tone suggesting the conversation was already over. "This is exactly the kind of real van life experience they want to see. Don't worry,

I'll make everyone look great and probably bring some of them here to boost local business."

The murmurs of discontent from other community members were becoming impossible to ignore. I caught fragments of conversations that revealed the depth of the problem: "didn't sign up to be content," "feels like being watched all the time," "what happened to asking for consent?" "my kids shouldn't be in stranger's videos."

Tank Williams had retreated toward his van, clearly uncomfortable with the prospect of being filmed without his permission. His hands shook slightly as he organized and reorganized his camp setup, the repetitive actions providing comfort against rising anxiety. A family with young children also hung back from the fire ring, the parents exchanging concerned looks about their kids appearing in a stranger's social media content without any control over how they might be portrayed.

"This is going to be a problem," Emmet said quietly, his law enforcement experience recognizing the signs of community tension approaching a breaking point.

"It already is a problem," I replied, watching more people notice Dakota's filming setup and decide to skip the community gathering entirely rather than risk unwanted exposure. "The question is what kind of problem it becomes."

Before Emmet could respond, the sound of a vehicle approaching too fast made everyone turn toward the meadow's entrance. A dusty pickup truck bounced over the rough access road, clearly being driven by someone in a hurry and not particularly concerned about the comfort of their suspension system or the safety of anyone who might be walking the informal paths between campsites.

The truck pulled up at the meadow's edge, gravel spraying and dust billowing in a cloud that drifted across several nearby campsites. An obviously agitated man climbed out, slamming the door hard enough that the sound echoed across the water and caused several children to look up from their games with startled expressions.

The man was probably in his fifties, with the weathered hands and permanent tan of someone who worked outdoors for a living in all kinds of weather. His work clothes were covered with field dirt and showed the wear patterns of someone who used tools daily and understood physical labor. But more than his appearance, his body language broadcast anger that had been building for some time and had finally reached the point where action became necessary.

Frank Brennan, I realized, recognizing him from town council meetings where he'd appeared to complain about various issues affecting local farmers. Drainage problems, zoning violations, teenagers using his property for unauthorized parties, and the dozen small irritations that accumulated when rural life collided with suburban expansion. His usual gruff demeanor had escalated to outright fury, and he strode toward the community fire with the single-minded determination of someone who'd reached the absolute end of his patience.

Dakota's eyes lit up as they spotted the approaching confrontation, and their entire demeanor shifted from casual documentation to predatory excitement. "Oh, this is perfect! Authentic local interaction content!" They swung their expensive camera toward Frank, apparently planning to document whatever was about to happen without any consideration for privacy or consent.

"Which one of you people has been trespassing on my property and damaging my crops?" Frank called out, his voice carrying across the meadow. "I want to know who thinks they can just help themselves to my land like it's some kind of public park."

The peaceful evening community gathering froze as Frank's anger crashed into the meadow's carefully maintained harmony. Parents instinctively pulled children closer, conversations died mid-sentence throughout the scattered campsites, and the crackling of the newly lit fire became the dominant sound besides Frank's heavy breathing and the electronic whir of Dakota's camera capturing it all for their followers' entertainment.

I looked at Emmet, recognizing the same realization in his eyes that I felt settling in my chest like a stone. Our peaceful meadow retreat had become much more complicated than we'd expected. The powder keg I'd sensed building all evening was about to explode, and Dakota was filming the fuse with obvious delight.

This was going to be interesting in all the wrong ways.

CHAPTER 2

Frank Brennan's anger radiated across the meadow like heat from summer pavement, his work boots crushing wildflowers as he stormed toward Dakota's elaborate filming setup. The camera lights cast harsh shadows across his weathered face, transforming familiar furrows into deep canyons of rage that spoke of sleepless nights and mounting financial pressure.

"Turn that damn camera off and listen to me!" Frank's voice boomed across the meadow, honed by decades of commanding attention over farm equipment and livestock. His callused hands clenched into fists at his sides. "Someone's been cutting through my fence and trampling my corn. Cost me hundreds of dollars in damage, and I want to know which one of you people thinks my land is some kind of public playground."

Dakota's response revealed everything I needed to know about their character. Instead of lowering the camera or showing basic human decency, they adjusted the angle for better composition, their eyes lighting up like a predator spotting wounded prey.

"This is exactly the kind of authentic local interaction that shows the real challenges of van life community building," Dakota announced to their camera, their voice taking on the performative tone I'd observed earlier. They turned toward Frank with calculated concern that looked genuine until you noticed the slight smile playing at the corners of their mouth. "Can you tell our viewers more about these alleged property damage issues?"

The word "alleged" hit Frank. His face flushed red beneath his permanent farmer's tan, and I watched his jaw muscles bunch as he fought to maintain control. Behind him, van lifers began gathering at a safe distance, drawn by the raised voices but clearly uncomfortable with being unwilling participants in whatever drama was unfolding.

"Alleged?" Frank's voice dropped to a dangerous growl. "I've got photos of trampled crops and cut fencing. I've got boot prints in my soil and garbage left where people camped without permission. That's not alleged, that's destruction of private property."

Dakota kept filming, apparently oblivious to how their behavior was escalating the situation. "So you're saying van lifers are inherently destructive to rural communities? That we can't coexist peacefully with traditional landowners?"

"That's not what I said at all!" Frank exploded, taking a step closer to the camera. His weathered hands shook with barely contained fury. "I said someone's been trespassing on my land and causing damage. I didn't say anything about all van lifers, but if you keep putting words in my mouth..."

"I'm just trying to understand your perspective," Dakota replied with fake sympathy that made my skin crawl. They angled the camera to catch Frank's mounting anger while maintaining their own expression of reasonable concern. "My followers deserve to know if local landowners are hostile to van life communities."

I felt sick watching Dakota manipulate the situation. They were using Frank's legitimate grievances as content, twisting his words to create a more dramatic narrative for their audience. Every leading question was designed to provoke a stronger reaction, and Frank was playing right into their hands.

River Martinez stepped forward. "Maybe we should all take a step back and let everyone cool down," he suggested, his voice calm but carrying unmistakable authority. "This seems like something that could be resolved through conversation rather than confrontation."

"Absolutely," Willow added, moving to River's side in perfect synchronization. Their years together had taught them to present a united front during community crises. "We could organize a community meeting to discuss property boundaries and make sure everyone understands what areas are off-limits."

But Dakota wasn't interested in resolution. They kept the camera rolling, capturing every moment of Frank's mounting frustration while maintaining their own façade of reasonable documentation. "Actually, this is public space, and I have every right to document what happens here. Freedom of the press protects authentic journalism, even when it makes people uncomfortable."

The casual dismissal of Frank's concerns and the community leaders' attempts at mediation revealed Dakota's true priorities. They weren't interested in being part of the van life community; they were interested in exploiting it for content that would drive engagement and grow their subscriber count.

Emmet moved closer to me, his law enforcement instincts recognizing the signs of a situation about to spiral out of control. "This is about to get ugly," he murmured.

Frank noticed Dakota was still filming and something inside him snapped. The careful control he'd maintained despite the provocation finally shattered, and I watched years of accumulated frustration pour out in a torrent of raw anger.

"You want content? Here's your content!" Frank jabbed a finger toward the camera, his voice rising to a roar that silenced conversations throughout the meadow. "If I catch anyone else on my property, I'm calling the sheriff and pressing charges for criminal trespass. And if any of you think you can just help yourselves to what I've spent my life building..."

He turned his attention directly to Dakota, his eyes burning with intensity. "And you! If I see that camera pointing at my land or my family, we're going to have a real problem. You understand me?"

Dakota's response was perfectly calculated to inflame the situation further. They lowered the camera just enough to make eye contact while keeping it recording, their expression shifting to wounded innocence. "Are you threatening me? Because my followers should know if local landowners are becoming violent toward van life communities."

The accusation of threatened violence was the final straw. Frank's weathered face went from red to purple, and for a moment I thought he might actually attack the camera. Instead, he turned and stalked toward his truck, his boots pounding against the earth with enough force to leave visible impressions in the soft meadow soil.

"I know who you are now," Frank shouted over his shoulder, his voice carrying across the entire campground. "And I'll be watching for you on my property! Try me!"

The truck door slammed with enough force to rattle the windows, and Frank peeled out in a spray of gravel that sent several nearby campers scrambling to protect their equipment. The dust cloud drifted across Dakota's filming setup, but they kept recording through it all, clearly delighted with the dramatic footage they'd captured.

"Perfect!" Dakota laughed once Frank's truck disappeared over the hill, their mask of concern dropping to reveal genuine excitement. "Nothing like authentic local color to show the real challenges van lifers face. That's going to get amazing engagement."

I realized Dakota was genuinely oblivious to how their behavior was affecting real people. They saw Frank not as a neighbor with valid grievances but as a character in their ongoing performance, useful only for the content value he provided.

Around the fire ring, other van lifers began expressing their discomfort with what they'd witnessed. Parents pulled children closer, their faces showing the strain of trying to explain adult conflicts that made no sense. Couples exchanged worried glances, clearly questioning whether they wanted to be part of a community where such confrontations were filmed for entertainment.

"I didn't sign up to be in someone's reality show," muttered an older woman near River's setup.

"None of us did," replied her partner, gathering their camp chairs with obvious intent to relocate away from Dakota's cameras. "This isn't what van life is supposed to be about."

River tried to salvage the situation. "Maybe we could have a community meeting about filming protocols," he suggested, his voice maintaining diplomatic calm despite the tension radiating from his shoulders. "Establish some ground rules that respect everyone's privacy and comfort levels."

Dakota dismissed the suggestion with casual arrogance. "You can't regulate authentic documentation. That's not how social media works. People choose to live publicly when they embrace van life. If they want privacy, they should stay in traditional housing."

The response sparked angry murmurs throughout the gathered crowd. These were people who'd chosen nomadic living for freedom and adventure, not to become unpaid actors in someone else's commercial enterprise. Dakota's assumption that public lifestyle meant consent to exploitation showed a fundamental misunderstanding of community ethics that most van lifers held sacred.

Tank Williams approached me, his military training evident in every economical movement despite the obvious tension radiating from his shoulders. His weathered face showed the hypervigilant expression I'd learned to recognize in veterans dealing with PTSD, and the confrontation had clearly triggered responses he was working hard to control.

"I've seen people like this before," Tank said quietly, his words heavy with hard-earned experience from places most people only read about. "They use everyone around them as props for their own story. They don't see other people as human beings, just as content opportunities."

Tank had described exactly what I'd been observing, but hearing it articulated by someone who'd seen manipulation and exploitation in life-or-death situations gave it additional gravity.

"It never ends well," Tank continued, his hands clenching and unclenching at his sides in a rhythm that suggested practiced stress management techniques. "People like that create their own problems. They just don't realize it until consequences catch up with them."

I noticed Dakota continuing to film "casual community interactions" without telling people the camera was running. They'd positioned themselves near the central gathering area where families were trying to salvage their evening routine, capturing conversations and activities without clear consent from anyone involved.

"Should someone say something?" I asked Tank, watching a family with young children realize they were being filmed and hastily retreat toward their RV.

"People have tried," Tank replied grimly. "But they've got an answer for everything. Legal rights, artistic freedom, promoting the lifestyle. They make it sound like you're the problem for wanting basic privacy."

Parents throughout the meadow began gathering their children with the protective urgency of people who'd realized their safe space had been compromised. The evening community gathering that had started with such promise was disintegrating as families retreated to their vehicles rather than risk unwanted exposure in someone else's social media content.

As the crowd thinned around the fire ring, a new figure approached Dakota's setup, her purpose unmistakable. The woman appeared to be in her early thirties, wearing professional outdoor gear that showed authentic wear patterns from actual adventure rather than careful styling. Her van setup was smaller but meticulously maintained, every piece of equipment serving a practical function rather than aesthetic appeal.

"We need to talk," she announced, barely

restrained fury crackling in her voice. "About the content you've been stealing from my channel."

Dakota initially pretended not to recognize the newcomer, but their defensive body language revealed the pretense immediately. "I'm sorry, do I know you?"

"Madison Swift," the woman replied, pulling out her phone. "Maybe my name rings a bell. Or maybe you know me better as 'MadAdventures' on YouTube and Instagram."

Recognition flickered across Dakota's face before they could suppress it, followed immediately by calculation. "Oh, right, I think I've seen some of your content. Small creator, right? Outdoorsy lifestyle stuff?"

The dismissive tone was clearly calculated to provoke, and Madison didn't disappoint. Her professional composure cracked enough to reveal the genuine hurt beneath her anger.

"Small creator whose ideas you've been systematically stealing," Madison shot back, her phone screen illuminating her face as she scrolled through evidence. "My 'authentic morning routine' concept that took me months to develop and perfect. You copied it frame by frame."

She turned the phone toward Dakota, showing side-by-side videos that made the theft undeniable. "Same music, same camera angles, same progression of activities. Even the same props and lighting setup. My subscribers are asking why I'm copying YOU when I posted the original content three weeks before your version went viral."

Dakota's response revealed their complete lack of shame about the appropriation. "Ideas aren't copyrighted. If you can't innovate fast enough to stay relevant, that's not my problem. The van life space is competitive, and success goes to creators who execute better."

"Execute better?" Madison's voice rose with genuine disbelief. "You mean execute with a bigger equipment budget and more professional editing? Because your 'better execution' is just my ideas with better production values."

The accusation hit close enough to truth that Dakota shifted tactics, moving from dismissal to attack. "Are you saying I stole from you? Because that sounds like defamation, and I record all my interactions for legal protection."

I realized Dakota was filming this confrontation just like they'd filmed Frank's anger, treating Madison's legitimate grievances as content opportunities rather than addressing the ethical issues she'd raised.

Madison noticed the camera and her anger intensified. "Of course you're recording this. You can't help yourself, can you? Everything has to be content for you."

"Nothing's private when you're living this lifestyle publicly," Dakota replied with casual cruelty. "You can't have it both ways, claiming you want to build a brand while demanding privacy when it's convenient."

"I never agreed to be in your content!" Madison's professional composure finally shattered completely. "And I sure as hell didn't agree to have my ideas stolen and my sponsors poached!"

The mention of sponsors revealed the deeper layer of Dakota's predatory behavior. This wasn't just about creative theft; it was about economic warfare against smaller creators who lacked the resources to compete with Dakota's production values and subscriber count.

"You reached out to three of my sponsors last week, didn't you?" Madison continued, her voice shaking with barely controlled fury. "Told them you could provide better engagement rates and more professional content for the same product placement fees?"

Dakota's slight smile confirmed Madison's accusation more clearly than words could have. "Business is competitive. If your sponsors prefer working with creators who can deliver better results, that's market dynamics, not theft."

"My channel was just starting to support my

van life," Madison said, her voice breaking as desperation overwhelmed her anger. "Those sponsor relationships took me two years to build. Now I might have to get a traditional job because you undercut my rates and convinced them I was amateur competition."

The human cost of Dakota's business practices became crystal clear in that moment. This wasn't abstract professional rivalry; this was someone's livelihood being destroyed by systematic predatory behavior. Madison had built something meaningful that allowed her to live her dreams, and Dakota was dismantling it for their own profit.

"You're destroying the community that welcomed you," Madison said, her anger giving way to heartbreak that was somehow more devastating to witness. "Van life used to be about cooperation and mutual support. People shared knowledge and resources because we understood we were all in this together."

She gathered herself for one final accusation that carried the weight of prophecy. "Eventually, people figure out who you really are. And when they do, you'll find out how it feels to be completely alone."

Madison stalked away toward her van, leaving Dakota alone with their camera and their complete inability to understand why anyone would be upset about their behavior. I watched them review the footage they'd just captured, clearly excited about the dramatic content rather than troubled by the genuine pain they'd caused.

As Madison disappeared into the growing darkness, another figure emerged from the shadows between vehicles. This person moved hesitantly, clearly nervous about approaching Dakota but compelled by desperation that overcame fear.

Jake Morrison appeared to be in his early twenties, wearing clothes that had once been expensive but now showed the signs of financial hardship. His van setup was visible nearby, a hastily converted cargo vehicle that looked more like someone's desperate attempt at housing than a lifestyle choice.

"Dakota?" Jake's voice held the trembling quality of someone begging. "Could I... could we talk for a minute? Please?"

Dakota's demeanor shifted instantly from professional content creator to cold personal cruelty. "I thought I made it clear we have nothing to discuss."

"I just want to apologize again," Jake pressed on, his hands shaking with nervous energy. "And ask if you'd consider taking down those videos from when we... from our relationship. Please."

The dynamic became immediately clear. This

was Dakota's ex-boyfriend, and whatever had happened between them had been documented and shared without his consent. Jake's obvious desperation suggested the consequences were still affecting his life in devastating ways.

"The breakup content performed incredibly well," Dakota replied, showing complete indifference to Jake's pain. "My subscribers love authentic relationship drama. Those videos have some of my highest engagement rates."

"But people recognize me now," Jake said, his voice cracking with humiliation. "I can't get work because employers google my name and find videos of me crying and begging. It's been six months, and it's still affecting my life."

Dakota's response revealed depths of cruelty I hadn't expected even from someone as selfish as they'd already proven to be. "You should have thought about that before you decided to be boring content. Relationships are supposed to grow and evolve. When they don't, there are consequences."

"Those videos make me look pathetic," Jake pleaded, tears gathering in his eyes. "You edited them to show only my worst moments, made it look like I was stalking you when I was just trying to save our relationship."

"I documented what happened," Dakota replied, radiating the self-righteousness of a true believer in their own propaganda. "If you looked pathetic, that's because of how you chose to behave, not how I chose to edit."

Jake tried a different approach, appealing to whatever human decency might still exist beneath Dakota's influencer persona. "I've been trying to rebuild my life. I moved out here to start over, but everywhere I go, people have seen those videos. They think they know who I am based on your version of our breakup."

"That's not my problem," Dakota said, pulling out their camera to begin filming this interaction as well. "Personal growth means taking responsibility for your choices instead of blaming others for documenting them."

Jake realized he was being filmed and instinctively covered his face, the gesture revealing just how deeply Dakota's previous content had traumatized him. "Please don't. I'm trying to rebuild my reputation. I can't handle more videos being posted."

"This is perfect follow-up content," Dakota announced to their camera, apparently addressing their audience. "The obsessive ex who can't move on, still trying to control my narrative months after we ended things."

The callousness was staggering. Dakota was using Jake's desperate attempt to reclaim his privacy as fresh content for their channel, perpetuating the cycle of exploitation that had already destroyed his employment prospects and social relationships.

"I'm not obsessive!" Jake protested, his voice rising with desperate frustration. "I just want to move on with my life without your videos defining me forever!"

"Then maybe you should have been better content," Dakota replied with devastating coldness. "My followers invest emotionally in my relationships. They deserve to see authentic outcomes, even when they're messy."

Jake retreated toward his van, his shoulders bent in defeat. He'd exhausted all hope of redemption. His shoulders shook with suppressed sobs, and I felt nauseated watching someone be systematically destroyed for the entertainment of strangers who would never understand the real-world consequences of their engagement metrics.

Other van lifers watched the confrontation in obvious discomfort, but none intervened. The bystander effect was in full operation, everyone assuming someone else would step forward while hoping they wouldn't become the next target of Dakota's documentary impulses.

"This is going to get amazing engagement," Dakota murmured while reviewing the footage, their excitement evident as they watched Jake's humiliation play back in high definition.

The pattern was becoming undeniably clear. Dakota moved through relationships and communities like a harvester, extracting content from every interaction while leaving damaged people in their wake. Frank's legitimate property concerns, Madison's financial stability, Jake's emotional recovery - all were secondary to the primary goal of feeding content to an audience that treated human suffering as entertainment.

I realized Dakota had created a trail of enemies through pure selfishness and cruelty. They seemed genuinely incapable of understanding how their behavior affected others, treating every person they encountered as a potential source of content rather than as human beings deserving basic respect and dignity.

Emmet moved closer to me, reaching the same conclusion. "That person has a lot of enemies," he said quietly. "And they're working hard to make more."

As the evening progressed, Dakota began preparing for their next content creation session with the obsessive attention to detail I'd observed earlier. They set up elaborate equipment for what they announced would be "authentic stargazing content," despite the late hour and the obvious exhaustion of everyone around them.

"I need everyone to move their outdoor lights," Dakota called to the remaining van lifers, as if their convenience was less important than cinematography requirements. "They're creating light pollution that interferes with the authentic night sky aesthetic."

The request was met with resigned compliance from people too tired to argue, but I noticed the resentment building in their expressions. Dakota was systematically alienating everyone who might have been willing to coexist peacefully, treating the shared space as their personal studio without regard for others' needs or comfort.

I overheard Dakota taking a phone call with someone who appeared to be their manager or business partner, their voice carrying clearly across the quiet meadow as they discussed strategy.

"The drama here is perfect for engagement," Dakota said, apparently reviewing the day's events like a satisfied business owner. "Rural versus nomadic lifestyle tensions, authentic community conflicts, real relationship fallout. My audience loves this kind of authentic documentation."

"I might stay longer than planned," Dakota continued, their voice rising with excitement. "This location is content gold. Tomorrow I want to film sunrise yoga and maybe get some more local interaction if that farmer comes back. The breakup follow-up content is testing really well with focus groups," Dakota went on, apparently discussing Jake's humiliation as a business strategy. "Audiences love relationship drama that feels authentic and unscripted."

River and Willow approached me as Dakota continued their business call, their faces showing the strain of trying to maintain community harmony in impossible circumstances.

"We've never had someone so disruptive to community atmosphere," Willow admitted, her optimism replaced by genuine concern. "Most people come here to be part of something bigger than themselves, but Dakota seems to see everyone else as supporting characters in their personal show."

"It's not sustainable," River added, his weathered hands clenching with frustration. "People are already talking about leaving early to avoid being filmed without consent. If this continues, we'll lose the community we've worked so hard to build. And I really love these people. This is our family now."

Their genuine distress highlighted the broader damage Dakota was causing. This wasn't just individual harm to Frank, Madison, and Jake; it was the systematic destruction of a functioning community that provided support and connection for dozens of people trying to live alternative lifestyles.

Tank Williams joined our conversation, his

military bearing more pronounced as stress activated old training responses. "People like that create their own problems," he said, echoing his earlier warning. "They just don't realize it until it's too late."

"What do you mean?" I asked, though I suspected I already knew the answer.

"They burn bridges without thinking about consequences," Tank explained, his eyes tracking Dakota's continued equipment setup. "Eventually they run out of people willing to tolerate their behavior. That's when they discover how dangerous isolation can be."

The ominous tone of Tank's observation sent chills down my spine. He wasn't making threats, though. He was making predictions based on patterns he'd observed in high-stress environments where social dynamics could mean the difference between survival and catastrophe.

Dakota finished their phone call and announced plans for their next content creation session. "I'm going to film some authentic nighttime van life content at that scenic oak tree," they called to anyone within hearing distance. "Sleeping under the stars with elevated perspective shots."

As if anybody cared…

They began gathering expensive climbing equipment, apparently planning to suspend cameras from the tree branches for dramatic angles. The elaborate setup required multiple trips from their van, and they worked alone since they'd alienated everyone who might have been willing to help.

"That seems dangerous," Emmet observed, watching Dakota struggle with professional-grade equipment that clearly required multiple people to operate safely.

"Everything they do seems dangerous," I replied, thinking about the trail of damaged relationships and destroyed trust Dakota was leaving behind them. "They just don't seem to realize it."

The remaining van lifers began retreating to their vehicles as Dakota's equipment setup created noise and light pollution that made peaceful evening activities impossible. Families gathered children early, couples abandoned romantic stargazing plans, and solo travelers gave up on the community connection that had brought them to the meadow in the first place.

"We should go," I said to Emmet, watching Dakota head toward the oak tree with equipment that would keep them filming long into the night. "This isn't the peaceful day we planned."

Emmet nodded, his expression reflecting the same disappointed recognition that our romantic retreat had been hijacked by someone else's drama. "Some people really know how to ruin a good thing."

As we gathered our picnic supplies and prepared to leave, I took one last look at the meadow that had been transformed from peaceful community gathering space into a film set for one person's ego-driven content creation. Dakota worked alone at the scenic oak tree, surrounded by expensive equipment but isolated from every human connection.

The van life community settled in for an uneasy sleep around them, their harmonious evening shattered by someone who claimed to represent their lifestyle while fundamentally misunderstanding everything it stood for. Children asked parents why the nice gathering had ended early, couples discussed whether they wanted to stay in a place where privacy and consent had become negotiable commodities, and solo travelers reconsidered whether community living was worth the risk of becoming unwilling content.

We drove away as Dakota tested lighting equipment that would illuminate their solo performance against the night sky, their excited chatter about camera angles and engagement metrics echoing across a meadow where they'd successfully alienated everyone who might have become friends, allies, or community members.

"Some people have to learn consequences the hard

way," came a voice from the darkness near Tank's van, though I couldn't identify the speaker.

The words followed us as we left the meadow behind, carrying the promise that Dakota's behavior would eventually catch up with them in ways they couldn't film, edit, or monetize for their audience's entertainment.

Tomorrow would bring whatever consequences Dakota had earned through their systematic destruction of community trust and individual dignity. The oak tree stood silhouetted against the star-filled sky, a natural monument.

As we drove toward home, I couldn't shake the feeling that we'd witnessed something more significant than simple social conflict. Dakota's behavior had created a perfect storm of resentment, financial desperation, and emotional trauma among people who'd come to the meadow seeking peace and community.

CHAPTER 3

My phone shattered the morning quiet with its urgent ringtone, Emmet's name flashing on the screen at an hour too early for casual conversation. Something in the timing sent ice water through my veins even before I answered.

"Dakota Rivers is dead." His voice carried the flat, professional tone he used when delivering news that would change everything. "I need you out here as supernatural consultant. Now."

The coffee mug slipped from my suddenly nerveless fingers, ceramic exploding against the kitchen floor in a spray of brown liquid and white fragments. After the drama we'd witnessed at the meadow the previous evening, I'd been grateful for the peaceful quiet of my own space, away from cameras and manipulation and systematic community destruction.

"What happened?"

"Climbing accident at the oak tree, but something feels wrong about the whole setup." His words came fast. "The scene looks too perfect, too staged. Like someone arranged it for maximum dramatic effect."

"Supernatural involvement?" I asked, already moving toward my bag.

"No obvious magic, I don't think, but there are too many convenient coincidences. Expensive camera equipment positioned to capture everything, but the memory cards are missing. Professional climbing harness that failed." Emmet paused, and I could hear voices in the background, radio chatter, the controlled chaos of a crime scene. "Someone wanted this to look like an accident, but they tried too hard to make it perfect."

My senses prickled as I processed the implications. "I'll be there in twenty minutes," I said. "Don't let anyone leave the scene until I've had a chance to analyze the situation."

"Already handled. The van life community is cooperating, but I can see the relief in their faces despite the shock. Whatever happened here, not many people are sorry it happened."

The drive to the meadow felt like traveling through a wormhole, the familiar landscape taking on ominous significance as I approached the scene of Dakota's final performance. Emergency vehicles filled the access road, their red and blue lights painting the morning air in harsh, artificial colors that clashed with the natural beauty of the rolling hills and wildflowers.

I parked behind Deputy Chen's patrol car and walked toward the oak tree where Dakota had planned their elaborate nighttime filming session. The massive tree stood like a silent witness, crime scene tape that fluttered in the morning breeze like prayer flags marking a sacred site.

The van life community had gathered in small clusters throughout the meadow, their quiet conversations creating a backdrop of barely suppressed tension. Parents held children closer than necessary, couples stood with protective body language, and solo travelers maintained careful distance from the investigation area. The appropriate expressions of shock and concern couldn't quite hide the underlying relief radiating from nearly everyone present.

Madison Swift stood apart from the main groups, her face a map of emotions that shifted between genuine surprise and something harder to identify. She kept glancing toward the oak tree with the fascinated horror of someone witnessing consequences they'd wished for but never expected to see manifest.

Jake Morrison looked like he hadn't slept in days, his clothes wrinkled and his eyes red-rimmed either from tears or exhaustion. He sat on the tailgate of his converted van, hands shaking as he stared at the crime scene with obvious devastation. Whether his reaction stemmed from grief, guilt, or simple shock was impossible to determine from his body language alone.

Tank Williams maintained his characteristic distance, but his military training was evident in how he observed everything while staying far enough away to avoid interfering with official procedures. His weathered face showed no emotion, but his eyes tracked every movement of the investigators with the hypervigilant attention.

Deputy Chen approached me as I reached the perimeter of the crime scene, her expression grim as she briefed me on the basic situation. "River Martinez found the body during his morning walk around six thirty. He called 911 immediately and began keeping other community members away from the scene."

"Time of death?"

"Coroner's preliminary estimate suggests sometime between midnight and 3:00 a.m., based on body temperature and rigor patterns. Dakota was alone, supposedly filming 'authentic nighttime van life content' according to multiple witnesses who heard equipment noise late into the night."

I extended my senses carefully, scanning the area around the oak tree for supernatural interference or residual magical energy. The reading came back clean. No supernatural entities had been involved in Dakota's death, no magical compulsions had influenced anyone's actions, no otherworldly forces had manipulated events for their own purposes.

But underneath the absence of supernatural influence, I detected something else entirely. Emotional residue clung to the oak tree and surrounding area like smoke from a recently extinguished fire. Fear, anger, and most disturbing of all, calculated intent. Someone had planned this very carefully, approaching the situation with cold intent rather than passionate rage.

"Where's Emmet?" I asked, noting that the sheriff was nowhere visible in the immediate crime scene area.

"Interviewing River Martinez about the discovery. He's pretty shaken up, finding bodies isn't part of his usual community leadership responsibilities." Chen gestured toward River and Willow's Airstream, where I could see Emmet taking notes while the older man spoke rapidly and gestured toward the oak tree.

I approached their conversation in time to hear River describing his morning routine and the discovery that had shattered the van life community's carefully maintained peace.

"I do my morning walk every day, check on folks, make sure everyone's okay," River explained, his weathered hands trembling slightly as he relived the experience. "Part of being unofficial community coordinator means keeping an eye on things, especially when we've got someone new who's been... disruptive."

"What did you expect to find at the oak tree?" Emmet asked, his notebook ready to capture every detail.

"Dakota filming, probably. They'd been setting up elaborate equipment for some kind of nighttime content session. I thought maybe I'd suggest they keep it quieter for the morning routine, be more considerate of people trying to sleep." River's voice cracked slightly. "Instead I found them tangled in that broken climbing harness, obviously dead. The equipment was still running, lights everywhere, but no sound."

Willow joined the conversation, her usual cheerful demeanor replaced by grim concern. "We heard the equipment noise until around two in the morning, then everything went quiet. Figured they'd finished filming and gone to sleep."

"Did you see anyone else moving around the oak tree during the night?" I asked, focusing on details that might reveal crucial information.

"That's the thing," Tank Williams said, approaching our group after apparently deciding his input was necessary. "I heard voices out there around midnight. Not just Dakota talking to their camera, actual conversation. Two people, maybe more."

The information sent electric tension through our small gathering. If Tank was correct, Dakota hadn't been alone when they died, which transformed this from a potential accident into definite murder investigation.

"Could you identify the voices?" Emmet asked, his pen poised to capture Tank's response.

"Negative. Distance was too great, and I was inside my van trying to sleep. But it definitely sounded like multiple people having some kind of discussion or argument. The conversation went on for maybe ten, fifteen minutes before the equipment noise picked up again."

Emmet and I exchanged meaningful glances. If Dakota had arranged to meet someone at the oak tree, or if someone had approached them during their filming session, the list of potential suspects narrowed dramatically to people Dakota trusted enough to be alone with in the dark.

"Let's examine the scene more closely," I suggested, noting that the coroner had finished preliminary work and the body had been removed. The oak tree stood draped in crime scene tape, but the area underneath was now accessible for detailed investigation.

The first thing that struck me as wrong was how perfectly positioned everything appeared. Dakota's expensive camera equipment formed a semicircle around the base of the oak tree, each device angled to capture different perspectives of what should have been a dramatic nighttime filming session. Ring lights created pools of illumination that would have made the area visible from significant distance, while backup cameras and audio equipment suggested elaborate production values far beyond casual documentation.

But despite the elaborate setup, crucial evidence was missing. Memory cards had been removed from every camera, their storage slots gaping empty like missing teeth. Dakota's phone, which they'd been surgically attached to during every moment I'd observed them, was nowhere to be found.

"Someone wanted to prevent us from seeing what really happened," I told Emmet, pointing out the systematic removal of recording devices. "This wasn't random theft. The equipment itself is worth thousands of dollars, but the perpetrator only took the items that contained evidence."

Deputy Chen joined our examination, her attention focused on the broken climbing harness that had allegedly caused Dakota's fatal fall. "This is professional-grade equipment, rated for climbers up to three hundred pounds. Dakota couldn't have weighed more than one-sixty soaking wet."

"Equipment failure can happen to anyone," Emmet said, but his tone suggested he didn't believe the convenient explanation any more than I did.

"Not like this." Chen held up sections of the harness that showed clear signs of deliberate sabotage. "These stress points were weakened systematically. Someone knew exactly where to compromise the webbing for maximum failure under minimum weight."

I knelt beside the oak tree, extending my senses to read the emotional residue that clung to the bark and roots like psychic fingerprints. The fear I detected was sharp and immediate. Dakota had realized they were in danger moments before the harness failed. But underneath that terror was something else: betrayal. They'd trusted whoever had been with them until the very last moment.

"Dakota knew their killer," I announced, standing and dusting off my jeans. "The emotional residue suggests someone they trusted enough to turn their back on, someone who used that trust to get close enough to sabotage the equipment."

"That narrows the field considerably," Emmet observed. "After yesterday's confrontations, Dakota didn't have many friends left in this community."

We spent the next hour conducting systematic interviews with every van lifer who'd witnessed

Dakota's behavior during the previous evening's community gathering. River and Willow repeated their account of trying to mediate Dakota's disruptive filming, their frustration evident as they described someone who'd refused every attempt at reasonable compromise. "We've built this community on cooperation and mutual respect," Willow explained. "Dakota seemed incapable of understanding that other people's comfort mattered as much as their content creation."

"Did they seem worried about personal safety?" I asked, searching for signs that Dakota had recognized the danger their behavior was creating.

"Just the opposite," River replied grimly. "They acted like the conflict was entertaining, like having enemies made them more interesting to their audience. They kept filming every confrontation instead of trying to resolve the underlying problems."

Madison Swift's interview revealed layers of resentment that went far deeper than professional rivalry. Her channel had been more than just creative expression. It was her lifeline to independence, her escape from traditional employment that would trap her in cubicles and conference rooms.

"I put everything into building that audience," Madison said, her voice tight as she struggled to control emotions that ranged from grief to relief. "Two years of consistent content, building relationships with sponsors, creating something meaningful that helped other women see van life as achievable. Dakota destroyed all of that in a matter of weeks."

"Did you consider confronting them privately?" Emmet asked.

"I tried. Multiple times. But every conversation became content for their channel. They'd film without telling me, then edit our discussions to make me look like a jealous competitor attacking their success." Madison's hands clenched into fists as she relived the systematic destruction of her professional relationships. "They turned my legitimate concerns into entertainment for their followers."

"Where were you last night between midnight and 3:00 a.m.?"

"Asleep in my van. Alone, unfortunately, so I can't prove it." Madison's honesty was either genuine or extremely well-rehearsed. "But I'll tell you honestly... I'm not sorry they're gone. The community will be healthier without their toxic influence."

Jake Morrison's interview was the most heartbreaking to witness. His hands shook throughout our conversation, and tears gathered in his eyes every time he tried to explain the depth of humiliation Dakota's content had caused him.

"Those breakup videos ruined my life," Jake said. "Employers google my name and find footage of me crying and begging. Dakota edited it to make me look pathetic, desperate, like some kind of stalker ex who couldn't accept reality."

"But you continued following their travel route," Chen observed, her tone carefully neutral.

"I was trying to rebuild. Van life was supposed to be a fresh start, somewhere I could be anonymous and figure out how to move forward." Jake wiped his eyes with a sleeve that had seen better days. "But everywhere I went, people recognized me from those videos. Dakota made sure I'd never escape what they'd documented."

"Did you approach them yesterday evening?"

"I tried. I thought maybe if I apologized again, if I explained how much damage those videos were causing, they might consider taking them down." Jake's laugh was bitter and broken. "Instead, they filmed my begging and called it follow-up content. They literally monetized my pain for their audience's entertainment."

"Where were you last night?"

"Sick. Food poisoning from some bad water I picked up three towns back. I was throwing up all night, couldn't have walked to the oak tree if I'd wanted to." Jake gestured toward his converted cargo van, which looked like the hasty work of someone who'd been forced into van life by circumstances rather than choosing it for adventure.

Tank Williams provided the most useful information despite his characteristic reluctance to get involved in community drama. His training had made him a keen observer of details others might miss, and his account of the evening's timeline was precise and detailed.

"I heard Dakota setting up equipment around 10:00 p.m.," Tank reported. "Lots of metal clanking, electronic equipment being tested, that distinctive whine of camera batteries charging. Normal routine for their filming sessions."

"When did you hear the voices?"

"Around midnight, maybe slightly after. Two distinct voices, possibly three, but the third one was quieter. Conversation lasted ten to fifteen minutes, then equipment noise resumed and continued until approximately 2:00 a.m."

"Could you determine the emotional tone of the conversation?"

"Negative. Distance and van walls prevented clear audio, but the rhythm suggested negotiation or planning rather than argument. No raised voices, no obvious conflict." Tank paused, considering his words carefully. "If I had to characterize it based on military experience, I'd say it sounded like a briefing or coordination meeting."

The information painted a chilling picture. Someone had arranged to meet Dakota at the oak tree, possibly under the pretext of helping with their filming or discussing the community conflicts from earlier in the evening. Dakota had trusted them enough to continue with their planned content session, unaware that their visitor was sabotaging the climbing equipment that would soon become their death trap.

As we wrapped up the initial interviews, several van lifers mentioned Frank Brennan's explosive threats from the previous evening's confrontation. His angry promises to "be watching" for Dakota and warnings about "real problems" if he saw cameras pointed toward his property had made a strong impression on everyone who'd witnessed the conflict.

"Frank was angrier than I've ever seen him," River admitted. "Farming's been tough on him since his wife died, and the trespassing problems were clearly the last straw. He made it very clear that Dakota should stay away from his land."

"He seemed genuinely dangerous," Willow added, her diplomatic nature struggling with the need to be honest about a neighbor's threatening behavior. "I've never seen him lose control like that before. Usually, he's gruff but reasonable."

Emmet made notes about Frank's obvious motive and public threats, marking him as the primary suspect who would require immediate investigation. "We'll need to verify his whereabouts during the relevant timeframe and determine whether he had opportunity to sabotage Dakota's equipment."

"He's the most obvious suspect," I agreed, but something about the convenient targeting made my investigative instincts twitch. "Skilled killers don't usually make public threats before committing murder. It's possible we're supposed to focus on Frank while the real perpetrator covers their tracks."

By late morning, the initial crime scene processing was complete. The coroner had removed Dakota's body for detailed autopsy. The broken equipment was bagged and tagged for forensic analysis that would either confirm or refute our suspicions about deliberate murder.

I briefed Emmet on my supernatural findings, confirming that no magical forces had been involved in Dakota's death but that the emotional residue suggested careful planning and calculated execution. "This wasn't a crime of passion," I concluded. "Someone approached this methodically, using Dakota's own filming routine and equipment against them."

Deputy Chen coordinated with the van

life community to ensure everyone remained available for follow-up questioning while allowing them to resume normal activities. The request to stay in the area was met without complaint. Most people seemed to understand that cooperation would resolve the situation faster than attempts to avoid involvement.

Madison Swift and Jake Morrison both seemed eager to leave the meadow and put the entire experience behind them, but they complied with the request to remain accessible for additional questioning. Madison packed her van, while Jake sat on his tailgate looking lost and overwhelmed by events that had spiraled far beyond his ability to process.

Tank Williams offered to help maintain community stability during the investigation period, his military background making him a natural choice for handling logistics and communication. "People are shaken up," he observed. "They need structure and leadership while processing what happened here."

As the official vehicles began departing and the meadow settled into an uneasy calm, I found myself studying the van life community that Dakota had tried so hard to exploit for content. Without their disruptive presence, the natural cooperation and mutual support that River and Willow had fostered began reasserting itself.

Parents let children resume normal activities while maintaining appropriate vigilance. Couples returned to planning their travel routes and sharing resources. Solo travelers began participating in conversations they'd avoided while Dakota's cameras were recording every interaction without consent.

The relief was evident, but it was complicated by the knowledge that someone among them had committed murder. The question wasn't whether anyone had reason to kill Dakota, but rather who'd possessed the means and opportunity to turn that desire into deadly action.

Standing beneath the oak tree where Dakota had staged their final performance, I understood that this investigation would require careful analysis of community dynamics, personal relationships, and the complex web of trust and betrayal that Dakota had woven through their exploitative behavior.

Someone had planned this very carefully, using Dakota's own methods and personality against them in a way that suggested intimate knowledge of their routines and vulnerabilities. The missing memory cards and phone indicated someone who understood how thoroughly Dakota documented their existence, someone who knew exactly what evidence needed to disappear to preserve their secret.

The van life community would never be quite the

same after Dakota's brief but destructive presence, but perhaps their death would allow the healing and rebuilding that their life had made impossible. River and Willow's vision of cooperation and mutual support could survive, if we could identify and remove the killer who'd taken justice into their own hands.

The meadow stretched around us like a crime scene painted in wildflowers and morning sunlight, beautiful and peaceful except for the knowledge that someone among its temporary residents had committed the perfect murder. Now we just had to figure out who'd been clever enough to turn Dakota's own narcissism into the weapon that destroyed them.

CHAPTER 4

Crime scene photographs hit the kitchen table with the sharp slap of revelations demanding attention. I spread them across the scarred wooden surface like tarot cards promising dark futures, each image capturing a piece of Dakota Rivers' final performance. Unlike their carefully curated social media content, these photos told a story of genuine terror and calculated betrayal.

"Emergency meeting," I'd texted an hour ago, and now my kitchen had transformed into a supernatural war room. The familiar chaos of my friends assembling always brought equal measures of comfort and anxiety. Comfort because I trusted these people with my life, anxiety because their presence meant something terrible had happened that required all our combined abilities to solve.

Opal arrived first, as always, her ginger curls catching the sunlight streaming through the windows as she bustled through the door with an armload of herbal teas and her characteristic determination to nurture everyone through crisis. She was so much like Lovage in that way.

Her rounded face showed lines of concern that aged her beyond her years, but her eyes held the fierce loyalty that had anchored our friendship since childhood.

"I felt it all the way across town," she said without preamble, setting her Thermos on the counter with shaking hands. "Someone died in pain and fear. The emotional echo is still vibrating through the supernatural atmosphere like a struck bell."

Bram thundered through the door next, his broad shoulders filling the doorframe as he carried what appeared to be half his ghost-hunting equipment. His bearded face was flushed with excitement and concern, hazel eyes bright with the childlike enthusiasm he brought to every paranormal investigation.

"I was conducting EMF readings near the cemetery when every piece of equipment started going haywire," he announced, dropping his gear with metallic clangs that made Origami rustle his paper wings nervously from his perch. "Whatever happened out there sent supernatural shockwaves through the entire area."

Angelica appeared in the doorway with uncharacteristic silent grace, her enhanced perceptions immediately scanning the room for threats and emotional undercurrents. The contamination from our previous supernatural encounter had left her abilities heightened but unpredictable, and I watched her pupils dilate slightly as she processed information beyond normal human senses.

Behind her, Jax materialized with that otherworldly quality that made him seem like he'd stepped through dimensions rather than walking up the front steps. His pale green eyes held old knowledge that contradicted his youthful appearance, and his shaggy sun-bleached hair moved in breezes that touched no one else. The guitar case slung across his shoulder suggested he'd come directly from his latest tour.

Lovage swept in last, her arms full of research materials and her laptop already open, fingers flying across keys as she accessed databases and social media accounts with the focused intensity that made her our most valuable information gatherer. Her linguistic abilities extended far beyond translation. She could read patterns in communication that revealed hidden truths about personality, motivation, and deception.

Aunt Hecate presided over our gathering from her chair by the window, but her attention seemed divided between our investigation and whatever obligations bound her to Malphas. The demon's influence cast subtle shadows across her features, and I noticed her fingers drumming patterns that looked suspiciously like binding sigils against the armrest.

"Dakota Rivers is dead," I announced without ceremony, watching each face process the information with varying degrees of surprise and recognition. "Found this morning at the oak tree in the meadow, apparently from a climbing accident that was definitely murder."

The silence that followed carried weight beyond shock. These were people who'd witnessed supernatural horrors and mundane tragedies, but something about Dakota's death resonated differently through our collective consciousness.

"I knew something was building toward violence in that meadow," Angelica said, her voice carrying the distant quality that marked her enhanced perceptions. "The emotional currents yesterday felt like a storm system about to break. Too much anger, too much desperation, too many people pushed beyond their breaking points."

I spread the crime scene photos across the table like pieces of a puzzle that would reveal Dakota's killer if arranged correctly. The images showed the oak tree draped in broken climbing harnesses, expensive camera equipment positioned for angles that captured nothing but darkness, and the conspicuous absence of memory cards that should have documented everything.

"Someone wanted this to look like an accident," I explained, pointing to specific details that had bothered me since discovering the scene. "But they tried too hard to make it perfect. Real accidents are messy and random. This feels orchestrated."

Opal reached for the evidence bags containing pieces of Dakota's climbing harness, her empathic abilities allowing her to read emotional imprints left on objects by intense experiences. I watched her face pale as she made contact with the webbing that had failed under suspicious circumstances.

"Oh," she whispered, her voice breaking with shared anguish. "They were genuinely terrified in those final moments. Not just scared of falling... betrayed. They trusted whoever was with them until the very end."

Her empathic reading confirmed my supernatural sense of the crime scene. Dakota hadn't died at the hands of a stranger or random attacker. Someone they considered safe had orchestrated their death with careful planning and calculated timing.

"There's more," Opal continued, her fingers trembling against the evidence bag. "The meadow is saturated with relief. Someone in that van life community is trying very hard not to feel guilty about being glad Dakota is dead. The emotion is so strong it's practically visible."

"Multiple someones," Angelica corrected, her enhanced perception allowing her to parse emotional signatures others might miss. "I noticed specific reactions yesterday that went beyond simple dislike. Madison Swift was watching Dakota with an intensity that suggested planning rather than passive observation. Jake Morrison's obsession has consumed his entire identity. Dakota's death might feel like liberation to him. And Frank Brennan's anger carries an edge of desperation that makes him capable of violence if pushed far enough."

Bram leaned forward, his expression growing serious as he contributed his observations from months of ghost-hunting investigations in the area. "I've been conducting paranormal research near that meadow regularly, which brought me into contact with the van life community. Dakota was like a virus infecting their social structure. Everything they touched became toxic."

He pulled out a notebook filled with detailed observations about community dynamics and individual behaviors. "Frank Brennan has been under tremendous pressure since his wife died. Medical bills, crop failures, the need to sell land to secure his daughter's college future. The van life presence is affecting his property values just when he needs every dollar he can get."

"How much pressure?" I asked, recognizing the signs of desperation that could drive normally reasonable people to extreme actions.

"Enough to make him consider options he'd never contemplate under normal circumstances,"

Bram replied grimly. "I've heard him talking to people in town about selling acres adjacent to the meadow, but potential buyers are concerned about liability issues with unsupervised camping. Dakota's disruptive behavior was making his financial situation worse every day they stayed."

Lovage looked up from her laptop screen, where multiple browser windows displayed Dakota's social media accounts, legal documents, and business registration information. Her linguistic analysis of communication patterns had revealed troubling information about Dakota's actual financial and legal status.

"Dakota wasn't nearly as successful as they appeared," Lovage announced, turning her screen toward the group. "Their subscriber count was artificially inflated with purchased followers, their actual engagement rates were declining, and they've been sued three times this year for copyright infringement and defamation."

She scrolled through a list of legal documents that painted a picture of systematic exploitation and financial desperation. "Multiple cease and desist orders from smaller creators whose content Dakota appropriated. Their business model was essentially parasitic. They'd identify successful creators with smaller platforms, copy their ideas with better production values, then poach their sponsors with claims of superior metrics."

"So they were desperate for viral content," I mused, understanding how that desperation might have driven Dakota to take increasing risks with other people's consent and safety. "Failing creators sometimes become more exploitative, not less."

"Exactly. And they were carrying significant debt despite their apparent success. Their van setup, equipment, and lifestyle were all financed through credit and sponsor advances they couldn't actually afford." Lovage's research had revealed the gap between Dakota's public image and private reality. "They needed constant content creation to stay ahead of their financial obligations."

Jax had been silent during our evidence analysis, but now he spoke with the otherworldly insight that made his observations unnervingly accurate despite their mystical delivery.

"That meadow is singing with discord," he said, his pale eyes focusing on something beyond normal perception. "Someone there is carrying a secret that's eating them alive, but it's not guilt over wrongdoing. It's pride disguised as shame."

His mystical awareness picked up emotional undercurrents that our more analytical approaches might miss. "Most people are lying about how they really felt about Dakota. The relief is too strong to be simple community healing after a disruptive presence. Whoever did this believes they saved everyone else."

"You're saying the killer thinks they're a hero?" Angelica asked, her enhanced perceptions resonating with Jax's mystical insights.

"That kind of self-righteousness leaves marks on the soul," Jax confirmed. "Whoever killed Dakota isn't struggling with guilt. They're struggling not to show how proud they are of solving everyone's problem."

The observation sent chills through our gathered group. Killers motivated by self-righteous heroism were often more dangerous than those driven by passion or greed, because they felt justified in their actions and might be planning additional "solutions" to perceived problems.

"All roads lead back to Frank Brennan," I said, organizing our evidence into a profile that law enforcement would find compelling. "Financial desperation, public threats, knowledge of equipment needed for the murder method, and clear opportunity during the night in question."

Bram nodded grimly. "His farming background includes extensive experience with ropes, harnesses, and load-bearing equipment. He might know exactly where to weaken climbing gear for maximum failure under minimum stress."

"And you said he made those threats in front of witnesses," Opal added, though her empathic reading suggested complicated emotions beneath the obvious evidence. "But something feels wrong about focusing only on Frank. The emotional signatures I'm picking up suggest multiple people were planning something, not just one angry farmer driven to violence."

Before we could debate Frank's guilt further, Emmet's arrival interrupted our analysis with the urgent energy that marked him transitioning from boyfriend to sheriff. His expression carried the grim satisfaction of evidence falling into place combined with the frustration of a case that felt too convenient to trust completely.

"We found Frank's business card in Dakota's van," he announced without preamble, setting evidence bags on our already crowded table. "Along with handwritten notes about a meeting to 'discuss property boundaries and mutual respect.'"

The physical evidence transformed Frank from obvious suspect to seemingly confirmed perpetrator. A planned meeting suggested premeditation rather than impulsive violence, and the location of the business card implied Dakota had expected to resolve their conflict through negotiation rather than confrontation.

"Security cameras in town caught Frank's truck heading toward the meadow around 11:00 p.m.," Emmet continued, consulting his notebook for exact details. "Timeline analysis puts him in the area during our estimated time of death."

"What about his alibi?" I asked, though the accumulating evidence made Frank's guilt seem increasingly inevitable.

"Claims he was home helping his daughter with college applications, but Emma was asleep by ten and can't verify his whereabouts after that. He lives alone, so no independent witnesses to confirm his story." Emmet's expression showed the satisfaction of an investigator watching pieces fall into place. "The case against Frank is circumstantial but building steadily."

"Too steadily," I muttered, my investigative instincts prickling at evidence that aligned so perfectly with the obvious narrative. "Real killers don't usually make it this easy to catch them."

"Sometimes they do when they're desperate and angry enough to stop thinking clearly," Emmet countered, though I caught the flicker of doubt in his expression that suggested he shared my unease about convenient evidence.

"The climbing harness was definitely sabotaged," he continued, showing us forensic photos that revealed cuts in webbing that would cause failure under stress. "Someone with knowledge of equipment failure points and access to appropriate tools. No fingerprints beyond Dakota's, which suggests the killer wore gloves and planned carefully."

As we reviewed the official evidence, our supernatural analysis began converging with law enforcement findings to create a compelling case against Frank Brennan. His motive was clear and urgent, his opportunity was established by security footage, and his expertise with equipment provided the means for murder.

"We need a coordinated investigation strategy," I decided, recognizing that our combined abilities could verify or disprove Frank's guilt more effectively than either approach alone. "Emmet schedules formal questioning with Frank tomorrow morning, with me present as supernatural consultant to detect deception. Angelica and Lovage continue researching other potential suspects," I continued, assigning roles that maximized our collective strengths. "We can't afford to tunnel vision on Frank if we're missing something important about Madison or Jake."

"I'll monitor community dynamics for signs of who might be hiding information," Bram offered, his ghost-hunting activities providing natural cover for ongoing surveillance. "Someone in that meadow knows more than they're admitting."

"And I'll keep listening to the songs the guilty sing when they think no one's paying attention," Jax added.

As our meeting wound down, I found myself staring at the crime scene photos with growing anxiety about the convenient path toward Frank's guilt.

"Real killers don't usually advertise their intentions beforehand," I said, voicing the doubt that had been growing throughout our analysis. "Frank made public threats, left his business card, and drove a distinctive truck past security cameras. Either he's incredibly stupid or we're supposed to focus on him while the real perpetrator covers their tracks."

"Or he's exactly what he appears to be," Emmet replied, though his tone suggested he was trying to convince himself as much as me. "Sometimes the most obvious answer is right, and sometimes desperate people make obvious mistakes."

"We'll know more after tomorrow's interrogation," I concluded, gathering the evidence photos into neat piles that would guide our next phase of investigation. "Frank's guilt or innocence should become clear once we can apply supernatural detection to his responses under pressure."

But as our team dispersed, I couldn't shake the feeling that Dakota's killer was counting on our focus remaining fixed on Frank Brennan's obvious guilt. The van life community held secrets beyond financial desperation and public threats, and someone among them had committed murder with enough skill to make it look accidental.

Origami fluttered restlessly on his perch as I turned off the kitchen lights, his paper wings rustling with the nervous energy that marked supernatural disturbances in our small town's carefully maintained equilibrium. Dakota Rivers had brought chaos to the van life community, but their death had brought something worse… a killer who believed they were a hero, and who might not be finished with their mission to save everyone from problems they'd appointed themselves to solve.

The crime scene photos lay stacked on my counter, waiting for a tomorrow that would either confirm Frank Brennan's guilt or force us deeper into the web of secrets Dakota had woven through the van life community. Someone had turned Dakota's own equipment and ego against them in a murder that masqueraded as accident, and tomorrow we'd begin discovering whether the real murderer was still hiding among the van lifers who'd welcomed our investigation with the relief of people finally free from a toxic presence they'd been powerless to remove.

Sometimes the most obvious answer was wrong, and sometimes it was exactly right.

CHAPTER 5

"Anything interesting in Dakota's personal effects?" I asked Emmet, watching the forensics team pack their equipment. The van life community maintained respectful distance, their morning coffee rituals subdued by the yellow tape that had transformed their peaceful gathering spot into evidence. Emmet was cataloging items. His expression carried the focused intensity that meant he'd found something significant.

"Receipt from a local camping supply store," he said, holding up a crumpled piece of paper protected in an evidence bag. "Rustic Trails Outfitters, purchased three days ago. Professional-grade climbing harness, rated for up to three hundred pounds."

The irony hit me like cold water. Dakota had bought the equipment that killed them from a local business, probably excited about creating "authentic" content with gear that seemed legitimate and safe. The receipt showed a price that reflected quality. This wasn't cheap equipment that might fail through normal wear, but expensive gear designed for serious climbers.

"Store's on Main Street," Emmet continued, consulting his notes. "Owner's named Sarah Beth Coleman. Been in business about five years, good reputation with the outdoor recreation crowd."

River approached our conversation, clearly wanting to help but not interfere with official business. His weathered face showed the strain of finding Dakota's body and then watching his peaceful community transform into a crime scene investigation.

"Coffee?" he offered, extending a Thermos that smelled like salvation. "Willow thought you folks might need caffeine before tackling whatever comes next."

"Much appreciated," I said, accepting the warmth gratefully. The morning air carried the bite of early autumn, and I'd been awake since Emmet's phone call shattered my peaceful sleep. "How's everyone holding up?"

"Shaken, but relieved," River admitted. "I know that sounds terrible, but Dakota was destroying what we've built here. People were starting to leave rather than deal with the constant filming and conflict."

"Anyone seem particularly upset about the death itself?" Emmet asked, probing for reactions that might indicate guilt or suspicious knowledge.

"Jake Morrison's been avoiding everyone since

yesterday morning. Won't answer questions, won't participate in community discussions about what happened." River's expression showed concern rather than accusation. "Could be grief, could be something else. Tank Williams mentioned Jake was acting nervous even before the body was found."

We'd need to follow up on Jake's behavior, but first I wanted to trace the equipment that had killed Dakota. The climbing harness represented the murder weapon, and understanding its source might reveal crucial information about premeditation and opportunity.

Rustic Trails Outfitters occupied a corner building on Main Street. The storefront windows displayed quality outdoor gear arranged with an eye for both function and aesthetic appeal, while hand-lettered signs advertised repair services and expert consultation.

The door chimed with genuine brass bells as we entered, and I immediately felt the organized competence of a well-managed inventory. Hiking boots, climbing gear, camping supplies, and technical clothing filled the space without creating claustrophobia, while price tags reflected the premium customers paid for equipment they trusted with their lives.

"Can I help you?" called a voice from behind the counter, and I turned to see a woman in her mid-forties approaching confidently. Sarah Beth Coleman looked like someone who'd spent serious time outdoors, but her business attire suggested equal comfort with commerce and customer service.

"Sheriff Quill, this is Sage Poe, my consultant," Emmet said, producing his badge and the evidence bag containing Dakota's receipt. "We're investigating the death of Dakota Rivers, and we understand they purchased climbing equipment from your store recently."

Sarah Beth's face shifted through shock, concern, and genuine distress as she processed the information. "That poor young person. I heard about the accident on the morning news, but I didn't realize they'd bought equipment here." She accepted the receipt with hands that trembled slightly, her reaction appearing completely authentic.

"I remember this sale," she said, consulting her computer system. "Three days ago, late afternoon. They were so excited about creating authentic camping content, asked lots of questions about weight ratings and safety protocols."

Her voice carried fond exasperation as she described dealing with enthusiastic but inexperienced customers. "I made sure they understood proper usage, gave them instruction sheets, even offered to demonstrate the setup.

They seemed genuinely interested in learning the right way."

"The equipment failed during use," I said, watching Sarah Beth's reaction carefully. My supernatural senses detected no deception, only growing concern and what appeared to be genuine shock at the implications.

"Failed?" Sarah Beth's voice rose with alarm that seemed entirely authentic. "That's impossible. This is professional-grade equipment from a manufacturer I've worked with for years. I've never had a failure report on this product line."

She pulled the climbing harness model information from her computer, scrolling through technical specifications and safety certifications. Her expertise with the gear she sold was obvious.

"Rated for up to three hundred pounds minimum, tested to over five hundred. Dakota couldn't have weighed more than one-sixty." Sarah Beth's growing distress appeared completely genuine as she contemplated the implications. "If this equipment failed during normal use, I need to contact the manufacturer immediately. They might need to do a recall."

"We'd appreciate your cooperation with the investigation," Emmet said, his tone suggesting official business rather than accusation. "Can you provide manufacturer contact information and any documentation about safety testing?"

"Absolutely," Sarah Beth replied, already pulling files from a well-organized cabinet. "I keep detailed records on all safety-critical equipment. If there's a defect in this product line, other customers could be at risk."

Her immediate cooperation and obvious concern for customer safety made a strong impression. This was someone who took equipment failure seriously, understanding that outdoor gear defects could literally kill people. My supernatural senses detected no deception, only the professional alarm of a businesswoman discovering that her products might be dangerous.

We left Rustic Trails Outfitters with manufacturer information, safety documentation, and my growing certainty that Sarah Beth Coleman was exactly what she appeared to be, a competent business owner horrified by the possibility that equipment from her store had caused someone's death.

"She seems genuinely shocked," Emmet observed as we walked back to our patrol car. "Either she's an excellent actress, or she had no idea that harness was going to fail."

"No supernatural red flags," I confirmed, though something about the entire situation continued bothering me in ways I couldn't articulate. "She reads as completely honest, professionally concerned, and appropriately helpful."

Our next stop was Frank Brennan's farm, where we planned to verify his alibi and search for evidence that might connect him to Dakota's death. The drive took us past rolling hills dotted with cattle and the kind of pastoral beauty that attracted tourists and van lifers seeking authentic rural experiences.

Frank's property showed the mixed prosperity and struggle typical of family farms in uncertain economic times. Well-maintained buildings and quality equipment suggested competent management, but deferred maintenance on non-essential structures revealed financial pressures that forced difficult choices about resource allocation.

Frank emerged from his barn as we approached, his expression wary. He'd clearly been expecting law enforcement attention. His weathered hands gripped a tool that could have been agricultural equipment or a weapon, depending on interpretation, and his body language radiated defensive hostility.

"Sheriff," he said, acknowledging Emmet with grudging respect while eyeing me with obvious suspicion. "Figured you'd be coming around eventually."

"Just need to verify some details about yesterday evening," Emmet replied, his tone carefully neutral. "Where were you between 10:00 p.m. and

2:00 a.m.?"

"Helping my daughter with her college applications until around ten, then she went to bed. Same as I told you before," Frank's response came readily, suggesting he'd been preparing for exactly this question. "After that, I was reviewing financial documents for a meeting with the bank next week. I spend most my nights reviewing financial documents these days."

"Anyone who can verify that?" I asked, extending my supernatural senses to read Frank's emotional state during questioning. His anger was genuine and intense, but underneath lay desperation and fear that spoke of someone pushed beyond his normal limits.

"Emma was asleep. I was alone with paperwork that's nobody's business but mine and the bank's." Frank's defensive tone suggested we'd hit sensitive territory about his financial situation. "But I never left my property after ten o'clock."

The lie hit my supernatural senses like a discordant note in an otherwise honest symphony. Frank was concealing something about his movements during the crucial timeframe, and his emotional signature showed the guilt of someone who'd done something he believed was justified but legally questionable.

"We have security footage from Murphy's Gas Station showing your truck heading toward the meadow at 11:47 p.m.," Emmet said, presenting evidence that contradicted Frank's claim about staying home.

Frank's weathered face flushed red with anger and embarrassment at being caught in deception. "All right, I drove out there. But I turned around without getting out of my truck. Decided it wasn't worth the trouble."

"Why did you go in the first place?" I pressed, sensing that Frank's explanation contained partial truth wrapped around significant omissions.

"Thought maybe I could reason with that kid about the trespassing problems," Frank said, frustration heavy in his voice. He'd clearly exhausted all reasonable options. "Figured if I approached them calm and private-like, we could work something out without involving lawyers."

His explanation sounded plausible, but my senses detected layers of planning and intent that suggested Frank's midnight trip involved more complex motivations than simple negotiation.

Emma Brennan appeared in the farmhouse doorway, a seventeen-year-old with her father's stubborn jawline and wise eyes that seemed older than her years. Her presence immediately shifted Frank's demeanor from defensive hostility to protective concern.

"Dad was helping me with my application essays

until ten," she confirmed, her voice carrying the honesty that made teenagers terrible liars but excellent witnesses. "Then I went to bed because I had a zero hour class this morning."

"Did you hear your father leave the house later?" Emmet asked gently, recognizing that Emma's testimony could either support or destroy Frank's revised alibi.

"No, but my room's on the back side of the house, and I sleep pretty heavily." Emma's answer was honest but unhelpful for establishing Frank's timeline. "He's been really stressed about money lately, staying up late working on financial stuff."

Frank's barn tour revealed exactly the kind of tools and knowledge that could be used to sabotage climbing equipment. Ropes, pulleys, and load-bearing hardware filled the workspace, while Frank's explanations demonstrated intimate familiarity with stress points and failure mechanisms.

"Thirty years of farming teaches you everything about what breaks and why," Frank said, unconsciously providing evidence of his capability to commit the crime. "Rope that'll hold a ton one day might snap under fifty pounds if it's been weakened in the right spot."

***

Back at the sheriff's office, forensic analysis

confirmed our growing case against Frank. His fingerprints on Dakota's van door handle, security footage placing him near the crime scene, and expert analysis showing tool marks that potentially matched equipment in his barn created a compelling narrative of premeditation and execution.

"The harness was cut with something like wire cutters," the forensic expert explained via phone, describing damage patterns that spoke of deliberate sabotage. "Someone knew exactly where to weaken the webbing for maximum failure under minimum stress. This wasn't random damage or normal wear. It was calculated to kill."

"Frank's got the knowledge and the tools," Emmet observed, reviewing evidence that seemed to point inevitably toward the desperate farmer's guilt. "Plus motive, opportunity, and a history of escalating threats."

"It feels too convenient," I admitted, my investigative instincts prickling at how perfectly the evidence aligned with the obvious suspect. "Real criminals usually make more mistakes, or fewer convenient ones."

We returned to the meadow for community interviews that supported our growing case against Frank. Madison Swift, River Martinez, and Tank Williams all confirmed Frank's escalating hostility and specific threats about "teaching these kids a lesson" if the trespassing problems continued.

"He seemed capable of violence that night," Madison said, her travel blogger instincts having noticed Frank's transition from frustrated neighbor to genuine threat. "The anger was different. It was more focused, like he'd made a decision about what needed to happen."

Tank Williams provided the most detailed observations about Frank's behavior during the previous weeks. "Frank was getting more desperate every day. Talked about taking matters into his own hands if legal options didn't work."

"He approached several van lifers directly, warning them about liability if someone got hurt on his property," Tank continued. "Seemed like he was building a case for justification rather than trying to prevent problems."

Sarah Beth accompanied us to the analysis when the forensics lab confirmed that Dakota's climbing harness had been deliberately sabotaged., her professional concern evident as the expert explained how someone with knowledge of equipment failure had turned quality gear into a death trap.

"This is my worst nightmare," Sarah Beth said, her voice shaking as she reviewed the forensic findings. "Someone used equipment from my store to commit murder. The liability implications could destroy my business, even if I did nothing wrong." Her reaction appeared completely genuine.

Back in town, research into Frank's financial situation revealed the desperate circumstances that provided compelling motive for extreme actions. Medical bills from his wife's cancer treatment totaled over $180,000, while declining farm income and rising costs had pushed him toward potential foreclosure.

"He needs to sell twenty acres to secure his daughter's college fund," the bank manager confirmed during our confidential inquiry. "But the van life presence is affecting property values and creating liability concerns that are scaring away potential buyers. Frank's been talking about those campers ruining his last chance at financial stability. Man's been under tremendous pressure since his wife died. That camping situation was the last straw."

As evening approached, I used my supernatural abilities to analyze the energy signatures around Frank's property and the crime scene. The emotional residue showed intense anger, desperation, and planning energy that supported the case against him, but something felt wrong about the supernatural signature.

"The energy suggests premeditation, but it's scattered," I explained to Emmet as we reviewed our findings. "Like multiple people were planning something, not just one angry farmer driven to violence."

The oak tree area showed clear evidence of fear, betrayal, and calculated violence, emotions consistent with Dakota's murder by someone they trusted. But the complex emotional landscape suggested layers of deception that went beyond Frank's obvious guilt.

"Frank is hiding something," I concluded, "but I'm not certain it's murder. The supernatural energy around him reads as desperate and angry, but not necessarily homicidal."

Despite my reservations, the physical evidence painted a compelling picture of Frank's guilt. Tool marks, timeline, motive, and opportunity all pointed toward the desperate farmer who'd made public threats and then been caught lying about his whereabouts during the murder.

"I'll bring him in soon for formal questioning," Emmet decided, reviewing evidence that would satisfy any prosecutor. "The case is circumstantial but strong enough for arrest if his responses indicate guilt."

As I drove home through the gathering darkness, I couldn't shake the feeling that Dakota's killer was counting on our focus remaining fixed on Frank Brennan's obvious guilt. The van life community held secrets beyond financial desperation and public threats, and someone among them had committed murder with enough skill to make Frank look like the perfect perpetrator.

The interrogation would either confirm Frank as our killer or force us to dig deeper into the complex web of relationships and motivations that had made Dakota Rivers so many enemies in such a short time. The meadow might look peaceful in moonlight, but someone among its temporary residents had planned the death, and they were watching our investigation with the satisfaction of someone whose misdirection was working exactly as intended.

Frank Brennan was desperate enough to commit murder, but so were other people whose financial and personal lives Dakota had systematically destroyed. The climbing harness had come from Sarah Beth's store, but the knowledge needed to sabotage it could have belonged to anyone with outdoor experience and access to basic tools.

CHAPTER 6

"I want my attorney present," Frank Brennan said, his weathered hands gripping the edge of the interview table in the sheriff's office. Emma sat beside him, her seventeen-year-old face pale, while a local lawyer shuffled papers with the nervous energy of someone handling his first potential murder case.

"That's your right," Emmet replied, settling into the chair across from Frank with the patient demeanor that made him effective at extracting truth from reluctant witnesses. "This is a formal interview regarding the death of Dakota Rivers. Sage Poe is here as our department consultant."

I positioned myself where I could observe Frank's reactions while extending my witch senses to read the emotional currents surrounding him. The supernatural energy radiating from the desperate farmer was complex, layers of anger, financial terror, and protective love for his daughter created a symphony of authentic human emotions.

"Tell us about your trip to the meadow the night Dakota died," Emmet began, his tone suggesting cooperation rather than accusation. "We have security footage showing your truck heading that direction at 11:47 p.m."

Frank's jaw tightened, but the truth spilled from his lips anyway, his shoulders sagging as the façade crumbled, his weathered face revealing the calculation that honesty might be his only remaining shield. "I drove out there, yes. But I never got out of my truck. Sat there for maybe thirty minutes, thinking about what I wanted to say, then decided it wasn't worth the trouble."

My supernatural senses detected partial truth layered with concealment. Frank was being honest about the basic facts while hiding specific details about his observations and intentions. The guilt signature suggested he'd done something he believed was justified but legally questionable... not murder, but something related to his property disputes.

"What exactly did you see during those thirty minutes?" I asked, focusing my abilities on Frank's emotional responses to determine whether his concealment related to witnessing the murder or committing it.

"Dakota's filming setup was running full blast. Lights everywhere, camera equipment scattered around that oak tree like some kind of movie production." Frank's description carried grudging admiration beneath his resentment. "I could see them moving around, setting up some kind of elaborate shot."

"Anyone else present?" Emmet pressed, recognizing the crucial importance of Frank's potential witness testimony.

Frank hesitated, glancing at his attorney before continuing with obvious reluctance. "Small van or converted car parked on the far side of the oak tree. Couldn't see much in the dark, but someone else was definitely there. Two people at least, maybe three."

The revelation sent electric tension through the interview room. If Frank was telling the truth, he'd witnessed the actual murder scene without realizing what he was observing. His testimony could identify Dakota's killer if we could verify his story and extract more detailed information.

"Can you describe the vehicle?" I asked, my supernatural senses confirming Frank's honesty about seeing additional people at the crime scene. His relief at finally telling this part of the truth was evident in the shift of emotional energy around him.

"Dark colored, smaller than Dakota's big van. Looked like one of those converted cars that some of the younger van lifers use when they can't afford the fancy setups." Frank's observation skills made him a more reliable witness than his emotional state might suggest. "Whoever it was, they knew Dakota well enough to approach during filming. No conflict, no argument that I could see."

"Why didn't you mention this earlier?" Emmet asked, though his tone suggested understanding rather than accusation.

"Because I was ashamed," Frank admitted, his voice cracking with emotion. "I sat there watching those people, thinking about confronting them, maybe making threats I shouldn't make. When I heard Dakota was dead, I figured you'd assume I'd done it, and mentioning I was there would only make things worse."

His attorney nodded approvingly at Frank's honesty, clearly believing his client's innocence. "Mr. Brennan drove home without approaching anyone. The security footage from his neighbor's farm shows his truck returning at 12:32 a.m., confirming he left the meadow before any violence occurred."

The timeline made Frank's witness status even more valuable. If he'd left around 12:30 a.m. and Dakota died between midnight and 3:00 a.m., Frank had observed the early stages of whatever meeting led to murder. His identification of a second vehicle provided our first concrete lead toward the real killer.

"We'll need a detailed statement about everything you observed," Emmet said, his demeanor shifting from interrogator to investigator gathering crucial evidence. "Vehicle description, number of people, any conversation you might have overheard."

"I'll cooperate fully," Frank replied, the relief evident in his posture as he realized we believed his witness testimony rather than suspecting him of murder. "That kid was destroying my financial future, but I'm not a killer. I'm just a farmer trying to protect my daughter's college fund."

My analysis confirmed Frank's fundamental honesty about the murder. His anger toward Dakota was genuine and intense, but the guilt signature suggested property-related deception rather than homicidal behavior. Whatever Frank was still hiding involved his ongoing conflicts with van lifers, not Dakota's death.

After Frank's interview, Deputy Chen briefed us on mounting pressure from the van life community and local business interests. Her expression showed the strain of managing a murder investigation while community tensions threatened to spiral beyond control.

"Half the van lifers are planning to leave early," Chen reported, consulting her notes. "They came here for peace and adventure, not to be part of a murder investigation. Parents are worried about their kids' safety, couples are arguing about whether to stay, and the solo travelers are getting nervous about camping alone."

"What about community leadership?" I asked,

recognizing that River and Willow's influence could either stabilize or accelerate the dissolution Chen was describing.

"River and Willow are doing their best to hold things together, but they're worried about complete community breakdown. People are starting to suspect each other, asking questions about who was where during the murder." Chen's report painted a picture of trust eroding under investigative pressure. "They've asked me to emphasize that solving this quickly would prevent permanent damage to van life culture in this area."

"Tourism board's also breathing down our necks," Chen continued. "Negative publicity about murders at popular camping spots could devastate the local outdoor recreation economy. They're pushing for quick resolution before the story goes national."

The time pressure was becoming critical. If the van life community scattered before we identified Dakota's killer, crucial witnesses might become unavailable and evidence could be lost. We needed to focus our investigation on the most promising leads while the community remained intact.

***

"Frank's testimony about a second vehicle changes everything," Emmet said as we walked back toward the meadow to continue gathering evidence. "We're looking for someone Dakota trusted enough to meet during their filming session."

"Someone from the van life community," I added. "Someone who knew Dakota's routines and filming schedule well enough to approach without causing alarm."

As we surveyed the meadow, I noticed a van setup that stood out from the others through its professional organization and quality equipment. The converted vehicle showed the careful modifications and gear selection of someone who understood outdoor life as both lifestyle and business opportunity.

"Professional content creator," I observed, noting the camera equipment, lighting gear, and climbing supplies arranged with the precision of someone who depended on this equipment for their livelihood. "Whoever owns this van knows what they're doing."

A woman emerged from the van as we approached. Madison Swift appeared to be in her early thirties. She had the weathered competence of someone who'd spent genuine time outdoors combined with the camera-ready grooming that marked serious content creators.

"Can I help you?" Madison asked, her tone friendly but cautious as she recognized our official status. "I'm Madison Swift. I heard about the terrible accident with Dakota Rivers."

"Sheriff Quill, this is Sage Poe, our department consultant," Emmet said, producing his badge while maintaining the conversational tone that put witnesses at ease. "We're investigating Dakota's death, and we're talking to everyone who was in the meadow that night."

"Of course," Madison replied, her expression shifting through appropriate shock and concern. "Such a tragedy. Van life community safety depends on proper equipment knowledge. Accidents like this shouldn't happen to experienced creators."

Her response triggered my supernatural attention. The emotional signature surrounding Madison carried layers of carefully controlled resentment beneath professional sympathy. She was managing her reactions with the skill of someone accustomed to performing emotions for audiences.

"You mentioned you're a content creator as well?" I asked, extending my senses to analyze the complex emotions radiating from this apparently helpful witness.

"MadAdventures on YouTube and Instagram," she confirmed, her voice carrying subtle pride mixed with underlying frustration. "Eighteen thousand subscribers focused on authentic outdoor experiences and gear education. I've been doing van life for three years now."

"Did you know Dakota personally?" Emmet asked. Though we both already knew the answer.

Madison's hesitation lasted only a moment, but it was enough for my supernatural senses to detect deception brewing beneath her helpful façade. "We were… professional acquaintances. The van life content creator community is pretty small. We'd interacted online and met a few times at gatherings like this."

"What was your impression of Dakota?" I pressed, sensing that Madison's carefully neutral description concealed much stronger feelings about her fellow creator.

"Talented," Madison said, her tone suggesting significant reservation behind the compliment. "Very good at creating engaging content that got impressive view counts. They understood what audiences wanted to see."

The diplomatic response revealed nothing while confirming everything. Madison's supernatural signature showed bitter resentment wrapped in professional courtesy. It was exactly what I'd expect from someone whose livelihood had been systematically undermined by Dakota's success.

"I imagine the content creation business is pretty competitive," Emmet observed, recognizing the potential for professional rivalry to escalate into personal conflict.

"More than people realize," Madison admitted, her guard dropping slightly as she warmed to a topic where she could express frustration without seeming suspicious. "Sponsorship opportunities are limited, and audience attention spans are short. When someone copies your concepts and executes them with better production values..."

She caught herself before completing the thought, but I picked up on the genuine pain beneath her words. Dakota hadn't just been competition. They'd been a direct threat to Madison's financial survival and creative identity.

"Dakota copied your content?" I asked, encouraging Madison to reveal the depth of conflict that might provide motive for murder.

"Systematically," Madison said, her professional composure cracking. "My 'authentic morning routine' series that took months to develop... Dakota reproduced it frame by frame with better cameras and editing. They contacted my sponsors, convinced them they could provide higher engagement rates for the same partnership fees."

"That must have been financially devastating," Emmet observed, recognizing the economic motive that could drive someone to extreme actions.

"Patagonia was my biggest sponsor," Madison confirmed, her voice tight with barely controlled frustration. "Two-year partnership that was supposed to fund my van life adventures and equipment upgrades. Dakota convinced them I was 'small-time amateur content' compared to their professional production values."

The financial impact was clearly severe. Madison's van setup showed quality gear but also the careful budgeting of someone operating on tight margins. Losing a major sponsorship would threaten her ability to maintain the lifestyle and equipment necessary for content creation.

"When did you lose the Patagonia deal?" I asked, my supernatural senses detecting the genuine desperation behind Madison's professional frustration.

"Three weeks ago," Madison replied, her timeline placing Dakota's systematic undermining of her livelihood in the immediate period before their death. "I've been trying to rebuild relationships with other sponsors, but Dakota's higher subscriber count and engagement metrics made me look like amateur competition."

"That must have been incredibly frustrating," I said, encouraging Madison to reveal more about her emotional state during the crucial period leading up to Dakota's murder.

"It was more than frustrating," Madison admitted, her carefully maintained composure finally cracking. "My channel was my only income source.

Losing major sponsorships was threatening to force me back to traditional employment like cubicles, conference rooms, everything I'd escaped by choosing van life."

Her motivation was becoming crystal clear. Dakota hadn't just been professional competition. They'd been systematically destroying Madison's financial independence and forcing her toward the conventional lifestyle she'd rejected. For someone who'd built their identity around nomadic freedom, that represented existential threat.

"Where were you the night Dakota died?" Emmet asked, shifting into direct questioning now that we'd established Madison's motive and opportunity.

"Here at the meadow, same as everyone else," Madison replied, but I detected evasion in her response. "I was planning content for the next day, reviewing footage, doing the technical work that audiences never see."

"Anyone who can verify that?" I pressed, noting the gap between Madison's claim of routine activities and the deceptive energy surrounding her alibi.

"I work alone most evenings. Part of the solo van life experience is learning to be comfortable with solitude." Madison's explanation sounded reasonable but provided no independent verification of her whereabouts during the murder timeframe.

"We noticed your van setup includes climbing equipment," Emmet observed, gesturing toward the professional-grade gear visible in Madison's storage compartments. "Do you have experience with the type of equipment Dakota was using?"

Madison's enthusiasm for the technical topic immediately revealed her extensive knowledge. "Absolutely. I research all my gear thoroughly—too many creators get hurt using cheap equipment or improper setup techniques. That's actually part of my channel's educational mission."

"Could you demonstrate proper climbing harness setup?" I asked, testing whether Madison possessed the expertise necessary to commit the sophisticated sabotage that killed Dakota.

"Of course," Madison replied, pulling equipment from her storage. As she explained proper usage, her technical knowledge became impressive and concerning. She understood stress points, failure mechanisms, and safety protocols with the expertise of someone who could easily identify vulnerabilities.

"This is exactly how you'd sabotage a harness if you wanted it to fail under stress," Madison said, pointing out specific weak points in the webbing. "Cut here and here, leave the rest intact, and it would support static weight but snap under dynamic loading."

Her casual demonstration of murder techniques was a bit shocking. Madison possessed the technical knowledge, equipment access, and bitter motivation necessary to kill Dakota with precisely the method used. I also detected deception surrounding her activities the night of the murder, suggesting she was concealing crucial information about her movements and actions.

"Whoever killed Dakota knew exactly what they were doing," Madison continued, apparently oblivious to how her expertise implicated her in the crime. "This wasn't amateur work. It required understanding equipment failure patterns and access to appropriate tools."

"Tools like what you have here?" Emmet asked, noting the wire cutters, knives, and other equipment that could easily sabotage climbing gear.

"Standard equipment for any serious van lifer," Madison replied, but her defensive tone suggested she recognized how her capabilities made her a suspect. "We all carry tools for equipment maintenance and emergency repairs. It would be foolish not to…"

***

Back at the sheriff's office, we analyzed Madison's story and found troubling gaps in her alibi. Her social media posts had stopped abruptly the night of Dakota's murder, resuming the next morning with typical content about van life adventures and gear recommendations.

"She goes offline sometimes when developing new content ideas," Chen reported after interviewing other van lifers about Madison's habits. "Claims she needs uninterrupted creative time without the distraction of social media engagement."

But phone records revealed suspicious activity immediately after Dakota's body was discovered. Madison had contacted sponsors and business partners within hours of the murder announcement, apparently calculating opportunities to rebuild relationships Dakota had damaged.

"I thought this might be an opportunity to reclaim partnerships they'd stolen," Madison had explained when questioned about the calls. "The van life content space would be less crowded without Dakota's aggressive business practices."

Her immediate business calculations about Dakota's death seemed callous at best, calculating at worst. Normal people might be shocked or grieving by a community member's violent death. Madison's first instinct was apparently strategic planning about reclaiming market share.

"Tank Williams confirms Madison has been part of the meadow community for several days," Chen continued, reviewing witness statements.

"But Zoe Parker mentioned something interesting about Madison's behavior around Dakota."

"What kind of behavior?" I asked, prickling with anticipation of crucial information.

"Madison was asking detailed questions about Dakota's equipment and filming schedule. When they usually started their evening sessions, what kind of gear they preferred, how late they typically worked." Chen's report painted a picture of predatory observation disguised as professional interest.

"That could be innocent networking," Emmet observed, though his tone suggested he found the pattern suspicious.

"Maybe," Chen replied, "but River Martinez recalls Madison making cryptic comments about consequences for stealing content. Something like 'eventually people who take what's not theirs face consequences.'"

The threatening undertone transformed Madison's questions from innocent curiosity into potential reconnaissance for murder planning. If she'd been systematically gathering information about Dakota's routines and vulnerabilities, it suggested premeditation rather than impulsive violence.

Other van lifers described Madison's growing bitterness about Dakota's success and increasingly pointed comments about content theft and unfair competition. Tank Williams mentioned seeing Madison watching Dakota's filming sessions from a distance, her expression intense.

"She seemed really interested in Dakota's setup and timing," Zoe Parker confirmed when questioned about Madison's behavior. "Asked me if I knew when Dakota usually finished filming, whether they packed up their equipment immediately or left it running."

The pattern of observation and information gathering strongly suggested Madison had been planning something involving Dakota's filming routine. Combined with her technical expertise, bitter motivation, and deceptive alibi, the evidence was building a compelling case for her guilt.

As evening approached, our team assessed the mounting evidence against Madison Swift. Her professional rivalry with Dakota had escalated into systematic financial warfare that threatened her livelihood and lifestyle. She possessed the technical knowledge and equipment necessary to commit sophisticated sabotage. Her presence in the meadow provided opportunity, while her evasive alibi and immediate business calculations after the murder revealed suspicious behavior.

"Madison fits the profile perfectly," Emmet concluded as we reviewed witness statements and evidence. "Means, motive, opportunity, and the kind of calculated planning that matches our crime scene."

"Her supernatural signature shows deception about her activities that night," I confirmed, my witch abilities having detected layers of concealment beneath Madison's helpful cooperation. "She's hiding something significant about her movements and actions."

"Frank's testimony about seeing a second vehicle supports the timeline," Chen added. "Small van or converted car matches Madison's setup, and the timing fits with her alibi gap."

Next, we'd bring Madison in for formal questioning, using both traditional interrogation techniques and supernatural analysis to determine whether our second suspect was actually Dakota's killer. The evidence was circumstantial but compelling. A professional rivalry, financial desperation, technical expertise, and suspicious behavior that suggested carefully planned murder.

But something about the case still bothered my investigative instincts. Madison's guilt seemed almost as convenient as Frank's had initially appeared. Two obvious suspects with clear motives and strong evidence, each more compelling than the last. Either we were building toward the right conclusion, or someone was very skilled at directing our attention away from the real killer.

The van life community was fracturing under pressure, time was running short before crucial witnesses scattered, and we needed resolution before more damage was done to both the meadow's peace and the local tourism economy. Madison Swift had the strongest motive and clearest opportunity of anyone we'd investigated.

Sometimes the most dangerous enemies were the ones who smiled while they planned your destruction. Tomorrow could reveal whether Madison's helpful façade had been concealing a murderer's calculating mind, or whether Dakota's real killer was still hiding among the van lifers who'd welcomed our investigation with the relief of people finally free from a toxic presence.

Madison Swift had every reason to want Dakota Rivers dead, and apparently, the knowledge and opportunity to make it happen.

CHAPTER 7

"We need to search Dakota's van," Angelica announced, bursting through the front door with the restless energy that marked her enhanced perceptions picking up something.... Who knew what... Her eyes held that distant quality that meant she was processing information beyond normal human awareness, and her agitation immediately put me on alert.

"The forensics team already went through it," I replied, looking up from the case files spread across the kitchen table. "They documented everything, photographed the interior, collected potential evidence."

"But they weren't looking for what we need to find," Angelica insisted. "I can sense deception layered throughout this entire investigation. Someone's going to beat us to crucial evidence if we don't act soon."

Her enhanced abilities had been increasingly reliable since the diner incident, but they also made her impulsive in ways that could complicate official investigations. I understood her urgency, but jumping ahead of proper procedures would create problems with Emmet and potentially compromise evidence for court proceedings.

"Let me call Emmet," I said, reaching for my phone. "If there's something specific we need to look for, he can arrange another official search with proper documentation."

Emmet answered on the second ring. "Please tell me you're calling with good news about our van life murder case."

"Angelica thinks we need to search Dakota's van again," I explained, watching my sister's agitated pacing increase as she waited for official permission. "She's sensing that someone might tamper with evidence if we don't act quickly."

"Absolutely not," Emmet replied without hesitation. "Forensics is planning another sweep tomorrow morning with specialized equipment for digital storage devices. We need to maintain proper chain of custody and documentation. I can't have civilian consultants conducting unauthorized searches."

"But what if..." I began, already anticipating Angelica's arguments about time sensitivity and supernatural insights that official procedures couldn't address.

"No buts, Sage. I know you trust Angelica's abilities, but this is a murder investigation that needs to hold up in court. Wait for the official search tomorrow."

I hung up feeling torn between professional responsibility and investigative instincts that agreed with Angelica's urgency. My sister immediately pounced on my conflicted expression with the persistence that made her impossible to ignore when she believed something was crucial.

"He said no, didn't he?" Angelica's enhanced empathy had probably detected my emotional response before I'd fully processed it myself. "Sage, my abilities are screaming that someone else is planning to search that van tonight. If we wait for official procedures, crucial evidence will disappear forever."

"Emmet has legal procedures to follow," I said, though my voice lacked conviction as I considered the implications of losing evidence that could identify Dakota's killer. "Chain of custody matters for prosecuting whoever murdered Dakota."

"What good is chain of custody if there's no evidence left to document?" Angelica pressed, her agitation increasing as she struggled to translate supernatural insights into logical arguments. "I can feel deception and planning energy around that van. Someone knows what we're looking for, and they're going to get there first."

Before I could respond, Aunt Hecate materialized from the living room where she'd been consulting with Malphas about supernatural obligations that seemed to consume increasing amounts of her attention. Her presence immediately shifted the family dynamic in ways that made my cautious approach seem unnecessarily timid.

"The girl's right," Aunt Hecate declared. "Sometimes proper procedures become barriers to justice when you're dealing with clever criminals."

"Aunt Hecate…" I began, recognizing the dangerous alliance forming between the two most impulsive members of my supernatural support system.

"Don't 'Aunt Hecate' me, child," she interrupted, her eyes flashing with the determination that had made her formidable before Malphas's binding complicated her abilities. "That van contains evidence that someone is desperately trying to destroy or hide. Your enhanced sister can sense it, and your investigative instincts know it's true."

The pressure of their combined conviction was becoming difficult to resist, especially when my own supernatural senses were detecting the same urgency Angelica described. Someone was planning something involving Dakota's van, and waiting for official procedures might indeed result in crucial evidence disappearing.

"Where's Lovage?" I asked, hoping my most cautious sister might provide a voice of reason to counter the reckless enthusiasm building in my kitchen.

"Research date at the university library," Angelica replied with obvious relief that our most diplomatically minded sister wasn't available to argue against immediate action. "She's tracking down historical precedents for supernatural consultation in murder investigations."

Without Lovage's careful analysis and peace making abilities, the balance of family opinion was tilting decisively toward action over caution. Aunt Hecate and Angelica represented the wild, instinctive side of witchcraft that trusted supernatural insights over legal necessities.

"Think about it logically," Angelica continued, pressing her advantage while I wavered between competing loyalties. "Forensics already documented the van's contents. We're not disturbing a pristine crime scene. We're looking for something specific that official searches might miss."

"Like what, specifically?" I asked, though I was already mentally preparing for the unauthorized search my family was obviously determined to conduct.

"The missing memory cards," Angelica said, her enhanced perception apparently providing specific insights about what evidence remained hidden. "They're still in that van somewhere, hidden in a place that looks innocuous but contains crucial information about Dakota's investigation into equipment failures."

The revelation sent electric tension through my supernatural senses. If Dakota had been investigating equipment failures and documenting safety violations, the missing memory cards might contain evidence about systematic problems that provided motive for murder beyond simple personal conflicts.

"Equipment failures?" I asked, recognizing that this angle could explain why someone had wanted Dakota's investigation permanently stopped.

"Dakota was building an exposé about counterfeit outdoor gear being sold to van lifers," Angelica explained, her enhanced abilities apparently picking up residual energy from Dakota's investigative activities. "Someone was selling dangerous equipment that could kill people, and Dakota had gathered evidence to prove it."

The implications were staggering. If Dakota had discovered systematic safety violations that threatened lives and businesses, their murder might have been committed to prevent exposure of criminal activity rather than resolve personal conflicts. The memory cards could contain evidence that would destroy someone's livelihood and potentially lead to criminal charges.

"Who was Dakota investigating?" I pressed, my investigative instincts fully engaged despite my concerns about unauthorized evidence gathering.

"That's what we need to find out," Angelica replied. "But whoever it is knows Dakota was building a case against them, and they're going to destroy the evidence if we don't get there first."

Aunt Hecate nodded approvingly at Angelica's reasoning, her expression satisfied. "Sometimes justice requires action that can't wait for proper channels, Sage. You know this in your bones."

The combined pressure of family conviction and my own investigative instincts finally overcame my respect for Emmet's procedures. If crucial evidence was about to be destroyed, unauthorized searching was preferable to letting Dakota's killer cover their tracks through official delays.

"Fine," I said, feeling a mixture of excitement and anxiety that marked decisions to bend rules for greater purposes. "But we're careful, we document everything, and if we find evidence, we figure out how to legitimize it for court proceedings."

"Absolutely," Angelica agreed, though her eagerness suggested she was more focused on discovery than documentation. "My enhanced perception will help us locate hidden items that normal searches might miss."

"And if anyone asks what we're doing?" I asked, already planning the careful approach that would minimize our exposure to legal complications.

"You're community members checking on Dakota's belongings out of respect and concern," Aunt Hecate suggested. "Perfectly innocent until proven otherwise."

***

The van life community had settled into evening routines when we approached Dakota's converted vehicle an hour later. Most people were gathered around River and Willow's central fire ring, sharing stories and planning the next day's activities with the forced normalcy of people trying to maintain community cohesion despite the murder investigation disrupting their peaceful gathering.

Dakota's van sat isolated within the crime scene perimeter, yellow tape fluttering in the evening breeze like warnings about the consequences of unauthorized access. The vehicle looked smaller and more vulnerable than it had during Dakota's elaborate filming sessions, stripped of the camera equipment and lighting that had made it the center of community attention.

"Enhanced perception's picking up residual energy from recent searches," Angelica whispered as we approached the van's rear doors. "Official investigators were thorough but focused on obvious evidence. They missed something hidden in plain sight."

"What kind of something?" I asked, extending my own senses to detect whatever Angelica's enhanced abilities were revealing about hidden evidence.

"Digital storage that doesn't look like digital storage," she replied, her voice carrying the certainty that came with supernatural insight. "Dakota was paranoid about their investigation being discovered, so they disguised crucial evidence as something innocuous."

The van's interior reflected Dakota's personality: meticulously organized equipment storage combined with casual chaos. It was the space of someone who lived in constant motion. Professional camera gear occupied custom-built compartments, while personal belongings were crammed into whatever space remained between technical necessities.

"Look for anything that could contain hidden digital storage," I suggested, beginning my systematic search through Dakota's possessions. "USB drives, memory cards, anything that looks deliberately concealed."

Angelica's perception guided her toward specific areas, but after twenty minutes of careful searching, we'd found nothing beyond the ordinary detritus of van life: charging cables, spare batteries, protein bars, and the accumulated possessions of someone who lived entirely on the road.

"The forensics team was thorough," I admitted, frustrated by our lack of discoveries. "If there were any hidden memory cards, they either found them or they were never here."

"Something feels wrong," Angelica said, her intuition detecting undercurrents she couldn't quite interpret. "There's deception energy around this investigation, but I can't pinpoint the source."

"Maybe we're looking in the wrong place entirely," I suggested, beginning to question whether the missing memory cards were even in Dakota's van. "What if whoever killed them already retrieved whatever evidence they were trying to hide?"

Angelica nodded, her frustration evident as her supernatural insights failed to provide the clear guidance we needed. "My abilities are picking up planning and concealment, but it's scattered. Like multiple people are hiding different secrets."

We continued searching for another ten minutes, checking compartments, examining equipment, and looking for anything the official investigation might have missed. But Dakota's van yielded no hidden treasures, no smoking gun evidence, no dramatic revelations about their killer's identity.

"We should go," I finally said, recognizing that our unauthorized search was accomplishing nothing beyond increasing our risk of discovery. "If there was crucial evidence here, it's either gone or hidden better than we can find."

Just as we prepared to leave, the sound of footsteps approaching from outside froze us in terror. Someone was walking directly toward Dakota's van, their pace deliberate enough to suggest they had specific business with the vehicle rather than just passing by.

"Crap," I whispered, recognizing that we were about to be caught conducting unauthorized searches in an active crime scene. "Get down and stay quiet."

We crouched behind Dakota's storage compartments as the footsteps came closer, my heart pounding with the knowledge that discovery would create serious problems with Emmet and potentially compromise the entire investigation. Through the van's tinted windows, I could see a figure approaching in the gathering darkness.

The footsteps stopped just outside the van's rear doors. I held my breath, praying that whoever was out there would move on without investigating further. Angelica's hand found mine in the darkness, she was probably picking up the nervous energy radiating from both of us.

A shadow moved across the window, someone clearly examining the van from outside. I felt intent and nervous energy from our unknown observer, suggesting they had specific plans involving Dakota's vehicle rather than casual curiosity.

The rear door handle rattled slightly, as if someone was testing whether the van was securely locked. My pulse quickened as I realized whoever was outside might be planning their own unauthorized search of the crime scene.

After what felt like hours but was probably only minutes, the footsteps resumed, moving away from the van toward other areas of the meadow. I waited until the sounds faded completely before daring to whisper to Angelica.

"We need to get out of here before they come back," I said, recognizing that our narrow escape was a warning about the risks of unauthorized investigation activities.

We slipped out of Dakota's van like shadows, moving quickly toward the edge of the meadow where we could disappear into the darkness without being observed by whoever had been examining the vehicle. My heart didn't stop racing until we were safely away from the crime scene and potential discovery.

"Did you sense who that was?" I asked Angelica as we walked back toward my car, the adrenaline of nearly being caught still making my hands shake.

"Nervous energy, guilt about something, and very

specific intent involving Dakota's van," she replied. "Whoever it was, they weren't just casually curious."

Our unauthorized search had revealed nothing useful about Dakota's murder, but it had confirmed that someone else was interested in examining the crime scene under cover of darkness. The question was whether that person was Dakota's killer returning to destroy evidence, or another suspect with their own secrets to hide.

The van life community settled into their evening routines around us, unaware that multiple people were conducting clandestine investigations in their murdered neighbor's personal belongings.

Tomorrow would bring new revelations about who had been lurking around Dakota's van and what they'd been planning to find or destroy. Our failure to discover hidden evidence was disappointing, but our narrow escape had revealed that the killer was still active, still worried about exposure, and still willing to take risks to protect their secret.

The memory card containing Dakota's final investigation remained missing, but someone clearly believed it still existed and posed a threat worth risking discovery to eliminate.

CHAPTER 8

"Excuse me, Sage?"

I turned from examining the trampled grass around Dakota's crime scene to find Jake Morrison approaching, his hands shoved deep in his pockets and his shoulders hunched against the morning chill. His converted cargo van sat nearby, a hastily modified vehicle that looked more like emergency housing than lifestyle choice.

"Jake, right?" I said, though my supernatural senses immediately detected nervous energy radiating from him like heat waves. "You're part of the van life community here."

"Yeah, I... I wanted to talk to you about Dakota." Jake's voice cracked slightly, and he cleared his throat before continuing. "I know we had our differences, but nobody deserves what happened to them. I want to help find their killer."

His eagerness felt forced, like someone rehearsing lines for an audition they desperately needed to pass. I extended my magic carefully, reading the emotional currents swirling around this nervous young man who claimed he wanted justice.

"That's generous of you," I replied, noting how Jake's anxiety spiked when I focused my attention on him. "What kind of help did you have in mind?"

"Well, I probably knew Dakota better than anyone else here," Jake said, his confidence growing as he warmed to the topic. "We spent a lot of time together before things went wrong between us. I understand their routines and habits pretty well."

"What kind of routines?" I asked, curious to see what insights Jake might offer from their past relationship.

"Dakota was very particular about their filming schedule," Jake explained, his nervous energy increasing as he volunteered information. "They always set up their night shoots around 10:00 p.m., never earlier. Said the lighting was wrong before then for the authentic camping aesthetic they wanted."

The specificity bothered me. Most people wouldn't remember exact timing details from a relationship that ended months ago, especially not the way Jake was demonstrating.

"They really loved that oak tree for content creation," Jake continued, apparently oblivious to how his detailed knowledge was affecting me. "Perfect angles for their 'sleeping under the stars' series, good lighting options, close enough to their van for equipment runs."

"You seem to know a lot about Dakota's recent filming preferences," I observed, detecting growing nervousness as Jake realized he might be revealing too much.

"We stayed in touch," he said quickly, his defensive tone suggesting this explanation was prepared in advance. "I followed their social media like everyone else. Dakota was always posting about their content creation process."

But even as Jake offered this reasonable explanation, my supernatural senses caught the lie underneath his words. He was concealing something significant about the source of his detailed knowledge.

"Dakota posted about preferring 10:00 p.m. filming times?" I pressed, recognizing that successful content creators rarely shared specific scheduling information that could compromise their safety or privacy.

Jake hesitated, apparently realizing his mistake. "Not directly. They mentioned it in... in texts sometimes. When we were still talking."

"What about their equipment preferences?" I asked, testing whether Jake's knowledge extended beyond publicly available information. "Did they post about technical gear choices?"

"Dakota was always having equipment problems," Jake said, his confidence returning as he moved into what felt like safer territory. "Like that failure at the river campsite two weeks ago. Really shook them up because the gear was supposed to be professional quality."

I honed inn on that. Dakota's carefully curated social media presence would never include equipment failures that might damage their professional reputation or discourage sponsors.

"Dakota posted about equipment failures?" I asked, my supernatural abilities detecting a spike in Jake's anxiety as he realized he'd revealed information that contradicted his claimed source.

"Not posted exactly," Jake backtracked, sweat beading on his forehead despite the cool morning air. "More like... they mentioned it privately. In conversation."

"What river campsite?" I pressed, recognizing that Jake's knowledge was becoming increasingly specific and increasingly suspicious.

"The one near Glacier Point, where they filmed that sunrise yoga series," Jake replied automatically, then caught himself as he realized he was providing details that suggested firsthand observation. "They talked about how the location was perfect except for the equipment issues."

"Jake," I said slowly, my senses confirming that every word was wrapped in deception, "how did you have conversations about specific camping locations when Dakota never mentioned staying in touch after your breakup?"

His nervous energy exploded into full panic as the logical inconsistencies in his story became impossible to ignore. "We... I mean... they posted about some of those places."

"The secluded spot with bad cell service that you mentioned?" I continued, watching Jake's face pale as he realized the trap he'd walked into. "How did you text about that location if there was no cell coverage?"

Jake's mouth opened and closed without producing sound, his brain apparently struggling to fabricate explanations for knowledge that could only come from physical presence.

"You were there," I said, my supernatural abilities confirming the truth beneath his desperate attempts at deception. "You were at these locations, weren't you? Following Dakota to these campsites."

"It's not what you think," Jake said, his voice breaking as his carefully constructed lies collapsed under logical examination. "I wasn't stalking them. I was trying to understand why they destroyed our relationship."

The confession was a little shocking. Months of systematic pursuit, concealed observation, and detailed documentation of another person's movements and vulnerabilities.

"How long have you been following Dakota's route?" I asked, my voice carrying the authority of someone who'd uncovered a dangerous truth.

"Since April," Jake admitted, his resistance crumbling as the weight of his deception became impossible to maintain. "But I wasn't hurting anyone! I just wanted to experience the same places, try to understand their perspective."

"You've been stalking your ex for five months?" I said, horrified by the scope of obsession Jake was revealing. "Camping at the same spots, documenting their activities, tracking their movements?"

"I kept notes about their patterns," Jake said. Whining like someone who believed their actions were justified despite obvious evidence to the contrary. "I thought if I understood their content creation process, maybe I could rebuild my own reputation."

The rationalization was pathetic and terrifying in equal measure. Jake had convinced himself that systematic stalking was legitimate research, that violating Dakota's privacy and safety was acceptable if it served his emotional needs.

"What kind of notes?" I pressed, recognizing that Jake's documentation could provide crucial evidence about premeditation and planning.

"Maps of their routes, timing charts for their filming schedules, analysis of their content themes and location choices," Jake listed, apparently proud of his thoroughness. "I have spreadsheets tracking their sponsor relationships, engagement metrics, even equipment preferences."

My supernatural senses recoiled from the depth of obsession Jake was describing. This level of observation went far beyond normal breakup processing into dangerous territory that suggested capability for calculated violence.

"You documented Dakota's equipment preferences?" I asked, recognizing that this knowledge could have been used to plan the sabotage that killed them.

"I thought maybe if I learned their methods, I could create content that would rehabilitate my image. I explained that already…" Jake said, his justification becoming increasingly desperate as he recognized how his behavior sounded when described aloud. "Those breakup videos ruined everything. My career, my social life, and my self-respect were all blown to pieces."

His emotional breakdown revealed the rage beneath his pathetic exterior. Jake's humiliation had metastasized into systematic pursuit and detailed planning that could easily escalate into violence.

"Where were you the night Dakota died?" I asked, feeling the dangerous potential in someone whose obsession had consumed months of his life.

"I was sick," Jake said quickly, his prepared alibi rolling off his tongue with practiced ease. "Food poisoning from bad water. Spent the whole night throwing up."

"Anyone who can verify that?" I pressed, though Jake's isolation and secretive behavior suggested he'd been alone during the crucial timeframe.

"No, I was by myself," he replied, then added details that immediately triggered my internal alert systems. "I heard the equipment noise stop around 2:00 a.m., then everything went quiet."

The information stopped me cold. Jake claimed to have been sick, but somehow he'd monitored Dakota's filming activities closely enough to know specific timing details about when equipment noise ceased.

"How did you hear equipment details if you were that sick?" I asked, recognizing that Jake's alibi contained logical inconsistencies that suggested much closer proximity to the crime scene.

Jake's face flushed red as he realized his mistake. "The meadow isn't that big. Sound carries at night, especially technical equipment noise."

But I felt the lie beneath his reasonable explanation. Jake had been much closer to Dakota's filming session than his alibi suggested, close enough to monitor timing and activities with the precision his stalking pattern had established.

"Jake," I said, "you've been following Dakota for months, documenting their every movement, and you happened to be camped close enough to monitor their equipment noise the night they were murdered?"

His nervous energy transformed into defensive hostility as he recognized that his lies were collapsing under examination. "You don't understand what it's like to have your life destroyed for content."

"So you destroyed theirs?" I asked.

"Those breakup videos followed me everywhere," Jake said, his voice rising with anger that had been building for months. "Employers googled my name and found footage of me crying and begging. Women rejected me for dates because they'd seen me looking pathetic online. I couldn't escape what Dakota had done to me."

The depth of his humiliation was staggering, but it provided compelling motive for someone capable of the systematic planning that Dakota's murder required. Jake had been watching, documenting, and obsessing over every detail of Dakota's life for months.

"Maybe Dakota's death was justice," Jake

continued, his mask of helpful cooperation finally slipping to reveal the dangerous resentment underneath. "For all the lives they destroyed for their audience's entertainment."

"Are you confessing to murder?" I asked, picking up on a volatile combination of rage, humiliation, and detailed knowledge that could easily have led to violence.

"I'm saying some people get what they deserve," Jake replied, his tone carrying cold satisfaction. "And maybe you should be careful about digging too deep into things that are better left buried."

The threat was unmistakable and immediate. Jake's nervous energy had transformed into aggressive defensiveness that suggested someone capable of violence when cornered.

"Is that a threat?" I asked, sensing that Jake's dangerous potential was now directed toward me.

"It's advice," Jake said, taking a step closer that felt distinctly menacing. "Dakota made a lot of enemies with their content. People who lost money, relationships, reputations because of what Dakota documented and shared. You should consider whether you want to join that list."

The implication was clear: continue investigating, and face the same consequences that had befallen Dakota. Jake's transformation from pathetic victim to genuine threat was complete, revealing someone whose obsession and humiliation had created capacity for calculated violence.

"We're done here," I said, recognizing that Jake's hostile energy was escalating toward physical confrontation. "Sheriff Quill will want to discuss your stalking activities and your proximity to the crime scene."

"Good luck proving anything," Jake said, his confidence returning as he realized he'd revealed his true nature. "Grief makes people say strange things. Maybe I was just confused about timeline details because I'm still processing the trauma of losing someone I cared about."

He was already constructing plausible explanations for his suspicious knowledge and threatening behavior.

Jake stalked back toward his converted van. His body language radiating satisfaction. He believed his threats had been effective. I watched him go.

The pattern was becoming impossible to ignore: Frank Brennan's financial desperation, Madison Swift's professional rivalry, and now Jake Morrison's obsessive stalking. Three perfect suspects, each with clear motive and compelling evidence, each more obvious than the last.

Someone was playing us, directing our attention toward convenient perpetrators while the real killer remained hidden among the helpful community members we'd barely considered threatening. But Jake's systematic stalking, detailed documentation, and weak alibi made him the most dangerous suspect yet.

His documented presence at multiple locations where Dakota had been, his intimate knowledge of their routines and vulnerabilities, and his threatening behavior when confronted created a compelling case for his guilt. Either Jake Morrison was Dakota's killer, or someone very skilled was using his obvious obsession to deflect attention from their own criminal activities.

The van life community continued their routines around us, unaware that one of their members had just revealed systematic stalking behavior and threatened the investigation. Jake's converted van sat among the peaceful gathering like a wolf among sheep, its owner possessing months of detailed planning and enough rage to kill for revenge.

CHAPTER 9

Mrs. Johnson clutched her purse against her chest as she entered the sheriff's office, her weathered face tight with nervous resolve. Three sleepless nights of debate had clearly preceded this moment. Gray hair escaped from her carefully pinned bun, and her sensible shoes squeaked against the linoleum as she approached Emmet's desk.

"I have something you need to see about Frank Brennan," she announced without preamble, setting a flash drive on his desk like evidence in a court case. "Security footage from my farm. Should have brought it sooner, but I didn't think it mattered until I heard you suspect him of murder."

Emmet accepted the drive while I moved closer to observe Mrs. Johnson's body language. Her emotional energy radiated honest concern mixed with guilt about delayed cooperation, but no deception about the evidence she was providing.

"What does the footage show?" Emmet asked, inserting the drive into his computer with the careful attention he gave to potentially crucial evidence.

"Frank's truck returning home at 12:32 a.m. the night that young person died," Mrs. Johnson replied, consulting a small notebook where she'd apparently recorded exact details. "Stays in his driveway all night. Never leaves again until morning when he does his usual farm chores around five-thirty."

The timestamp on the video confirmed her account precisely. Frank's distinctive pickup truck pulled into his driveway, headlights sweeping across Mrs. Johnson's camera range before disappearing behind his farmhouse. Hours of empty footage followed, showing the driveway remaining undisturbed until dawn brought normal farm activity.

"Camera covers the entire approach to his property?" I asked, recognizing that this evidence would either definitively clear Frank or reveal gaps that allowed alternative explanations.

"Only way on or off his land without crossing posted no-trespassing areas that would trigger motion sensors," Mrs. Johnson confirmed. "Been recording everything since teenagers started using back roads for their parties. Frank couldn't have left his property without my cameras catching it."

This was big news. Frank Brennan was innocent of Dakota's murder, transformed from our primary suspect into a crucial witness whose observations about the second vehicle now became central to identifying the real killer.

"This changes everything," Emmet said, reviewing the footage timestamps that established Frank's definitive alibi. "His testimony about seeing another vehicle at the crime scene becomes witness evidence instead of suspect misdirection."

Mrs. Johnson departed with our gratitude and assurances that her delayed cooperation wouldn't affect the investigation. Frank's clearance required immediate adjustment of our suspect focus, though the logical targets remained Madison Swift and Jake Morrison, both possessing compelling motives and suspicious behavior during our investigation.

"Madison's professional rivalry and Jake's obsessive stalking both provide clear motives," I said, organizing our evidence into the streamlined focus that Frank's elimination created. "Question is which of them moved from resentment to murder."

"Both had opportunity, both demonstrated relevant knowledge," Emmet agreed, though his tone suggested the same underlying unease that had been bothering my investigative instincts. "Almost too convenient how perfectly they fit the suspect profile."

Before we could delve deeper into analyzing our

remaining suspects, Sarah Beth Coleman appeared in the sheriff's office doorway, her expression bright with what appeared to be genuine relief about recent developments.

"I heard through the business association that Frank Brennan has been cleared," she said, approaching our desk with confident strides. Official settings clearly didn't intimidate her. "Such wonderful news. I was worried about having a dangerous person threatening the van life community."

Her concern seemed authentic, matching the civic-minded business owner who'd been helpful throughout our investigation. But something about her immediate knowledge of Frank's clearance triggered my attention. News traveled fast in small towns, but Sarah Beth's detailed information suggested active monitoring of investigation progress.

"The van life community will feel much safer knowing the threatening farmer wasn't responsible," Sarah Beth continued, settling into a chair without invitation. "I imagine this allows you to focus on the real perpetrators among the actual van lifers."

"What makes you think the killer is among the van lifers?" Emmet asked, noting the assumption underlying Sarah Beth's comment.

"Well, who else would have detailed knowledge

of Dakota's routines and equipment?" Sarah Beth replied with logic that seemed reasonable on the surface. "Plus access to their filming schedule and trust necessary to approach during a content session."

Her reasoning made sense, but I detected something rehearsed about her response, as though she'd prepared these talking points rather than forming them spontaneously.

"I'd be happy to provide additional assistance now that you've eliminated the obvious threat," Sarah Beth offered, her eagerness to remain involved becoming increasingly noticeable. "My equipment expertise might help identify which van lifer had the technical knowledge to sabotage climbing gear."

"That's generous," I said, extending my magical awareness to analyze the emotional currents surrounding Sarah Beth's helpful demeanor. "Do you have insights about specific community members?"

"That Madison Swift has extensive technical knowledge," Sarah Beth said immediately, her response coming too quickly for genuine consideration. "I've seen her discussing climbing equipment with other van lifers. Very knowledgeable about stress points and failure mechanisms."

The speed of her accusation bothered me,

particularly since Sarah Beth had no apparent basis for suspecting Madison beyond general equipment knowledge that multiple community members possessed.

"What about the crime scene itself?" Emmet asked, testing whether Sarah Beth would reveal knowledge beyond what had been shared with her officially. "Any thoughts about how the killer approached Dakota that night?"

Sarah Beth's eyes brightened with interest that seemed excessive for someone peripherally involved in the investigation. "Well, based on what I've heard, Dakota was expecting to film for several hours that night. The missing memory card from their main camera suggests they captured something they didn't want made public."

The detail stopped my breath cold. Information about the missing memory cards had never been discussed publicly or shared with civilian witnesses. Other than me discussing it with my sisters, but they wouldn't have told Sarah... Sarah Beth shouldn't know anything about what evidence was or wasn't found during the official searches.

"Where did you hear about the camera positioning?" I asked, my magical perception detecting a spike in controlled anxiety beneath Sarah Beth's helpful façade.

"Oh, you know how these things spread through

the community," Sarah Beth said with practiced vagueness. "People talk, especially about dramatic events like this. I probably heard it from one of the van lifers who was discussing the tragedy."

But her explanation felt hollow, lacking the specificity that would accompany genuine secondhand information. My mystical instincts warned that Sarah Beth possessed direct knowledge rather than community gossip.

"The timing is interesting too," Sarah Beth continued, apparently unaware that she was revealing suspicious familiarity with case details. "From what I understand, Dakota's filming equipment went silent around 2:00 a.m., which suggests the killer struck during a planned break in their content creation."

Well, that was something. The timing of when Dakota's equipment noise ceased had never been shared publicly. Only Frank had mentioned hearing the silence from his truck, and possibly Jake from his claimed position nearby. Sarah Beth had no legitimate source for this specific detail.

"Community members mentioned the timing?" Emmet asked, his tone carefully neutral despite the significance of Sarah Beth's revelation.

"Well, people piece things together," Sarah Beth replied, but her defensive posture revealed her recognition that she'd revealed information she shouldn't possess. "Sound carries in the meadow at night. I'm sure several people noticed when the noise stopped."

Her justification grew weaker with each word, particularly since Sarah Beth's store was miles from the meadow and she'd never claimed to be present during Dakota's murder. The knowledge she was demonstrating required either direct observation or inside information about the investigation.

"Have you been following the case closely?" I asked, detecting carefully controlled responses rather than the natural reactions I'd expect from an innocent business owner.

"Professional interest," Sarah Beth said with renewed confidence. "Equipment from my store was involved, so I need to understand what happened for insurance and liability purposes. The manufacturer wants detailed information about the failure circumstances."

Her business explanation sounded logical, but it didn't account for knowledge about crime scene staging, timing details, or investigation findings that extended far beyond equipment-related concerns.

"Speaking of equipment," Sarah Beth continued with enthusiasm that seemed forced, "I've been researching similar failure patterns to help prevent future tragedies. Did you know that climbing harnesses can be compromised in ways that make failure nearly undetectable until stress testing?"

The technical knowledge she was demonstrating extended well beyond normal retail expertise into territory that suggested hands-on experience with equipment sabotage methods. Her research on exactly how climbing gear could be weaponized became increasingly concerning.

"How much do you know about deliberate equipment failure?" Emmet asked, recognizing the same suspicious expertise that was bothering my investigative instincts.

"Enough to help customers avoid dangerous gear," Sarah Beth replied, but her tone carried defensive undertones. "Part of responsible business ownership is understanding product vulnerabilities and safety limitations."

"You seem particularly knowledgeable about sabotage techniques," I observed, watching Sarah Beth's emotional signature shift toward controlled anxiety despite her maintained helpful demeanor.

"Unfortunately, necessary knowledge in today's liability-conscious business environment," she said with what appeared to be genuine regret. "Insurance companies require detailed understanding of how equipment might fail and whether business owners could be held responsible."

Her explanation was reasonable enough to deflect suspicion while providing cover for suspicious technical expertise. But my perception continued detecting deception beneath her helpful cooperation.

"The investigation should probably focus on resolving things quickly," Sarah Beth said, shifting toward what seemed like her real agenda for this conversation. "Prolonged uncertainty hurts everyone - the van life community, local businesses, tourism interests. People need closure and confidence in outdoor recreation safety."

Her emphasis on rapid case resolution felt urgent in ways that exceeded normal business concerns. Sarah Beth seemed personally invested in seeing the investigation concluded promptly, suggesting stakes beyond community welfare.

"Are you concerned about specific business impacts?" Emmet asked, probing whether Sarah Beth's urgency stemmed from financial pressures related to the murder investigation.

"All outdoor recreation businesses suffer when people start questioning equipment safety," Sarah Beth replied with what appeared to be genuine concern. "Plus, the longer this drags on, the more likely tourists will choose different destinations for their adventures."

The reasoning was sound from a business

perspective, but combined with her suspicious knowledge and excessive helpfulness, it suggested someone monitoring investigation progress for personal rather than community reasons.

After Sarah Beth departed with renewed offers of assistance and reminders about the importance of quick resolution, I sat in contemplative silence while processing the troubling implications of our conversation.

"Something's wrong with her story," I told Emmet, my magical awareness having detected layers of deception beneath Sarah Beth's helpful business owner persona. "She knows details about the crime scene that were never made public."

"Camera positioning and timing information," Emmet agreed, consulting his notes about what evidence had been shared publicly versus kept confidential. "No legitimate way for her to know those specifics."

"Her helpfulness feels rehearsed rather than genuine," I continued, trying to articulate the mystical impressions that suggested careful preparation rather than spontaneous cooperation. "Like she's monitoring our progress instead of simply offering community support."

"Think she's involved?" Emmet asked, though his tone suggested reluctance to suspect someone who'd been consistently helpful throughout our investigation.

"I think we've been focusing on obvious suspects while the real killer hides among people we considered trustworthy," I replied, my investigative instincts finally crystallizing around the pattern that had been bothering me since the beginning. "Frank, Madison, Jake - all perfect suspects with clear motives and compelling evidence."

"Too perfect?" Emmet suggested, recognizing the same convenient progression of obvious perpetrators that had made our investigation feel almost scripted.

"Someone's been directing our attention toward convenient targets while staying invisible among the helpful community members," I concluded, my witch abilities confirming that Sarah Beth's emotional signature contained deception and personal investment that extended far beyond civic responsibility.

Sarah Beth Coleman had approached us as a helpful business owner concerned about community welfare, but her knowledge of confidential case details and rehearsed responses revealed someone with personal stakes in investigation outcomes.

Three obvious suspects had captured our attention while the fourth remained invisible among those we trusted most. Sarah Beth's mask was beginning to slip, revealing calculation beneath helpfulness and personal investment beneath community concern. The helpful store owner who'd sold Dakota the equipment that killed them possessed knowledge she shouldn't have and urgency she couldn't adequately explain.

For the first time since Dakota's death, I hoped we were looking in the right direction

CHAPTER 10

River Martinez's harness snapped without warning.

One moment he was demonstrating proper climbing technique to a group of concerned van lifers, the next he was sprawling in the dirt beside the oak tree where Dakota had died. The equipment failure occurred at minimal stress levels that should never have compromised quality gear, sending shock waves through the gathered crowd.

"Everyone, stay back!" Willow called out, rushing to help her husband while other community members stared in horror at the broken webbing scattered around River's feet. "Don't touch anything until the authorities examine it."

I arrived at the meadow within minutes of Emmet's radio call, my pulse racing as I processed the implications of this second equipment failure. River sat propped against the oak tree, shaken but uninjured thanks to the low height of his demonstration. His weathered face was pale with the realization of how close he'd come to serious injury.

"Same failure pattern as Dakota's harness?" I asked Emmet, who was already photographing the broken equipment with the focused attention the situation demanded.

"Identical cuts," he confirmed grimly. "Someone sabotaged this gear using the exact same technique that killed Dakota. This wasn't coincidence or manufacturing defect."

Tank Williams approached our examination area, his military bearing more pronounced than usual as stress activated old training responses. "River bought that harness from Sarah Beth's store three days ago," he reported. "Brand new, professional grade, rated for way more stress than a simple demonstration would create."

The information sent ice through my veins. Sarah Beth had sold River the equipment that nearly killed him, just as she'd sold Dakota the harness that succeeded in ending their life. The pattern was becoming impossible to ignore or explain through coincidence.

"We need to warn everyone about their gear," Madison Swift said, her voice tight with fear as she examined her own climbing equipment with newfound suspicion. "If someone's systematically sabotaging equipment from local stores, none of us are safe."

Her concern reflected the growing panic spreading through the van life community. Parents were gathering their children closer to their vehicles, couples were having urgent conversations about leaving immediately, and solo travelers were checking and rechecking their essential safety gear with obvious anxiety.

"How many people have purchased equipment from Rustic Trails Outfitters?" I asked the assembled crowd, recognizing that we needed to assess the scope of potential danger.

"Half the community, at least," Zoe Parker replied, her young face showing the strain of someone whose adventure lifestyle had suddenly become life-threatening. "Sarah Beth's store is the only outdoor gear supplier within fifty miles. Most of us have bought something there."

The revelation that Sarah Beth had equipped much of the van life community with potentially sabotaged gear created immediate crisis. Equipment that people depended on for safety during outdoor adventures could now be weapons waiting to fail at critical moments.

"Everyone needs to stop using any gear purchased from Rustic Trails until we can have it professionally inspected," Emmet announced, his sheriff's authority providing structure to the community's growing fear. "Safety first, investigation second."

Jake Morrison had been notably absent from the emergency gathering, but he approached our group now with obvious reluctance and nervous energy that immediately triggered my magical awareness. His converted van sat isolated at the edge of the meadow, and his behavior suggested someone wrestling with information they were reluctant to share.

"I need to tell you something," Jake said, his voice cracking with stress. "About Sarah Beth and her equipment sales. I think Dakota was investigating her business practices."

"What kind of investigation?" I asked, my witch abilities detecting truth mixed with fear in Jake's emotional signature.

"Dakota asked me questions about gear failures in other van life communities," Jake explained, his hands shaking as he recounted conversations he'd apparently been concealing. "They wanted to know if I'd heard about climbing equipment breaking when it shouldn't, or if other outdoor gear stores had unusual numbers of customer complaints."

Jake paused, gathering courage before continuing with information that clearly troubled him. "Dakota had been documenting equipment failures across multiple van life communities for months. They showed me photos of broken harnesses, failed carabiners, and climbing gear that snapped under normal use. All of it was supposed to be premium equipment, but the failure patterns suggested inferior materials."

"What made them suspect counterfeit gear specifically?" I asked, recognizing that this level of investigation required more than casual observation.

"Dakota had been comparing serial numbers and manufacturer markings on failed equipment with genuine products," Jake replied, his voice growing stronger as he shared information he'd clearly been wrestling with. "They discovered that some gear had fake certification stamps and counterfeit manufacturer logos. The metal composition was wrong, the stitching patterns didn't match genuine products, and the packaging had subtle differences from authentic items."

The revelation transformed our understanding of Dakota's investigation from abstract safety concerns to concrete evidence gathering about specific criminal activity. They hadn't stumbled across Sarah Beth's operation by accident, but had systematically traced counterfeit equipment back to its source.

"Did Dakota connect this to Sarah Beth's store?" Emmet pressed, though the answer seemed increasingly obvious.

"They were building a map of where the counterfeit equipment was being sold," Jake continued, pulling out his phone to show us screenshots he'd apparently saved from Dakota's research. "Multiple van lifers had purchased failed gear from the same regional suppliers. Rustic Trails Outfitters appeared on the list more than any other retailer."

The phone screen showed a detailed spreadsheet documenting equipment failures, purchase locations, and manufacturer verification attempts. Dakota had been conducting a thorough investigation that would have provided definitive proof of systematic counterfeit equipment sales throughout the region.

"Dakota planned to release this exposé in three parts," Jake explained, scrolling through additional documentation. "First, the scope of counterfeit gear in outdoor recreation. Second, the safety implications and injury patterns. Third, identification of the retailers and suppliers responsible for distributing dangerous fake equipment."

The investigation connected directly to Dakota's planned exposé about counterfeit outdoor gear. They hadn't just been investigating abstract safety violations, but had systematically documented specific problems tied to Sarah Beth's business practices and could prove her operation was putting lives at risk.

"Did Dakota suspect Sarah Beth specifically?"

Emmet pressed, recognizing the crucial importance of establishing what the victim had discovered before their death.

"They never said her name directly," Jake replied, "but they were very interested in equipment failure patterns and warranty claim processes. Dakota kept asking about whether manufacturers ever got suspicious about too many defect reports from specific retailers."

Emmet's phone rang before Jake could elaborate further, interrupting our discussion with the urgent tone that marked official investigation business. The district attorney's office had been monitoring the original murder case through law enforcement channels, and their patience was wearing thin.

"Sheriff Quill, we need resolution on this case immediately," the DA's voice carried through Emmet's phone speaker with crystalline authority. "Community safety concerns and tourism impact require immediate arrest of the responsible party in the Rivers murder."

"We're building evidence against a specific suspect," Emmet replied carefully, balancing the pressure for rapid action with the need for prosecution-quality proof. "But we need concrete evidence before making arrests."

"The van life community is planning mass exodus from the area," the DA continued. "Tourism board is reporting cancellations from other outdoor recreation groups who've heard about the murder. This situation is affecting regional economic stability."

The external pressure for quick resolution was becoming overwhelming, but rushing the investigation could compromise our ability to prove Sarah Beth's guilt in court proceedings. We needed definitive evidence that would survive legal challenges while protecting the community from additional sabotaged equipment.

After ending the call with promises of rapid progress, Emmet and I retreated to his patrol car to contact the manufacturers whose information Sarah Beth had so helpfully provided during our initial investigation. The irony wasn't lost on me that her cooperation was now leading directly to evidence of her criminal activities.

"This is regarding the climbing harness involved in a fatality in your area," Emmet explained to the manufacturer's customer service representative. "We need to verify warranty and defect claim histories for equipment sold through Rustic Trails Outfitters."

The initial response was professional but cautious, as expected when dealing with product liability issues that could affect both manufacturer reputation and legal exposure. However, when Emmet mentioned that we were investigating systematic equipment failures and potential fraud, the conversation's tone shifted dramatically.

"Please hold while I connect you with our warranty fraud department," the representative said, her voice heavy with gravity. She'd clearly encountered this type of problem before. "We've had concerns about unusual claim patterns from that retailer."

The warranty fraud investigator who picked up our call had clearly been expecting contact about Sarah Beth's business practices. His response to our inquiry was immediate and detailed, suggesting that an investigation had been building for some time.

"Rustic Trails Outfitters has generated the highest number of warranty claims of any retailer in our network," the investigator explained with obvious frustration. "Over the past two years, they've submitted claims for defective equipment totaling nearly $40,000 in manufacturer reimbursements."

"Is that unusual for a retail location?" I asked, though the investigator's tone suggested the answer was obvious.

"Extremely unusual," he confirmed. "Most retailers might submit one or two legitimate warranty claims per year. Sarah Beth Coleman has averaged one claim per month, all for expensive equipment that allegedly failed during normal use."

The pattern was becoming clear, but the investigator's next revelation transformed our understanding of Sarah Beth's criminal enterprise completely.

"The real problem is that we have no record of selling most of this equipment to Rustic Trails Outfitters," he continued, his voice carrying the anger of someone who'd discovered systematic fraud. "She's been submitting warranty claims for gear we never manufactured or sold to her, collecting reimbursements for counterfeit equipment that she's selling as genuine products."

The pieces fell into place with devastating clarity. Sarah Beth had been purchasing cheap counterfeit climbing gear and selling it at premium prices while maintaining the facade of a legitimate outdoor equipment retailer. When the inferior counterfeit equipment failed and injured customers, she filed fraudulent warranty claims with real manufacturers, collecting reimbursements for gear she'd never actually purchased from them. The scheme had worked for years because warranty departments rarely cross-referenced claims with sales records from other divisions - corporate silos that Sarah Beth had exploited to avoid detection until the pattern became too obvious to ignore.

"She's running a counterfeit equipment operation," I said, my voice tight with the implications for community safety. "Selling fake gear at real prices, then blaming manufacturers when people get hurt."

"And collecting double profits," Emmet added grimly. "Markup from selling cheap counterfeits as premium gear, plus fraudulent reimbursements from manufacturers she's never done business with."

The financial motive for Dakota's murder was now crystal clear. Dakota's planned exposé about counterfeit outdoor gear would have uncovered Sarah Beth's criminal enterprise, resulting in criminal charges, business closure, and personal financial ruin. The missing memory card undoubtedly contained evidence of Sarah Beth's fraud that would have supported Dakota's investigation.

"How much money are we talking about?" Emmet asked the warranty investigator.

"Based on our records, she's collected over $40,000 in fraudulent reimbursements over two years," came the reply. "But that's just from our company. If she's running the same scam with other manufacturers, the total could be much higher."

Sarah Beth's struggling business had been kept afloat through systematic fraud that put customers at deadly risk while generating substantial illegal profits. Dakota's investigation threatened to expose the entire operation, providing compelling motive for murder that went far beyond professional rivalry or personal conflicts.

"We need to examine Sarah Beth's store inventory immediately," Emmet told me as we processed the magnitude of her criminal activities. "If she's selling counterfeit equipment to the van life community, there could be dozens of people carrying gear that might fail at critical moments."

The ongoing danger to community safety was becoming our primary concern, even beyond proving Sarah Beth's guilt in Dakota's murder. River's near-miss demonstrated that she was continuing to sell dangerous equipment despite the investigation, suggesting either desperation or complete disregard for human life.

"She's escalating rather than lying low," I observed, my magical perception detecting the dangerous patterns emerging from Sarah Beth's behavior. "Most criminals would stop their illegal activities during a murder investigation, but she's continuing to sell potentially lethal equipment."

"Which means she's either completely confident she won't be caught, or she's too desperate to stop," Emmet replied, recognizing the implications for our investigation strategy. "Either way, she represents an immediate threat to anyone using gear from her store."

We returned to the meadow to find the van life community in the early stages of evacuation preparation. Families were packing essential equipment while examining their climbing gear with obvious suspicion, couples were having urgent discussions about alternative destinations, and solo travelers were posting warnings on social media about potential equipment safety problems in the area.

"We can't let everyone scatter before we resolve this," I said, watching the community that had provided Dakota's social context beginning to dissolve under pressure from ongoing safety threats. "If Sarah Beth is continuing to sell dangerous equipment, these people need protection, not just warnings about avoiding her store."

"Plus, we need witnesses available for prosecution," Emmet added, balancing community safety with legal necessities. "Half our evidence comes from van lifer testimony about Sarah Beth's behavior and business practices."

The challenge was protecting the community from additional sabotaged equipment while gathering evidence for criminal prosecution and preventing Sarah Beth from destroying documentation that proved her fraudulent activities. Her business operated from a physical location filled with inventory and records that could provide definitive proof of her criminal enterprise.

"We need surveillance on Rustic Trails Outfitters," I said, recognizing that Sarah Beth's next moves could determine whether we gathered enough evidence for prosecution or lost our case to evidence destruction. "If she realizes we're building a case against her, she might try to destroy records or flee."

"Already coordinating with state investigators," Emmet confirmed, his phone buzzing with messages from law enforcement agencies now taking interest in the case. "But we need to move fast. Every hour we delay gives her more opportunity to cover her tracks."

The investigation had transformed from solving Dakota's murder to preventing additional deaths while building a case against a criminal enterprise that threatened outdoor recreation safety throughout the region. Sarah Beth's counterfeit equipment scheme represented systematic fraud that could have injured or killed dozens of people beyond Dakota and River.

"She's been hiding behind a helpful business owner persona while running a criminal operation that turns safety equipment into potential weapons," I said, my witch abilities confirming the dangerous calculations driving Sarah Beth's behavior. "Dakota's investigation threatened to expose everything, so she eliminated the threat."

"And now she's trapped," Emmet observed. "Can't stop selling equipment without arousing suspicion, can't flee without abandoning her business, can't destroy evidence without making herself look guilty."

The van life community gathered around River's failed equipment represented both potential victims of Sarah Beth's ongoing criminal activities and crucial witnesses to her behavior patterns. Their safety depended on our ability to neutralize the threat she posed while preserving the evidence needed for criminal prosecution.

Sarah Beth Coleman had been selling death disguised as safety equipment, collecting profits from both the initial fraud and subsequent manufacturer reimbursements while customers risked their lives with gear designed to fail. Dakota Rivers had discovered this criminal enterprise and paid with their life for threatening to expose it.

The helpful store owner who'd been cooperating with our investigation was actually the killer we'd been seeking, hidden behind a facade of civic responsibility while operating a criminal enterprise that treated customer safety as expendable in pursuit of illegal profits.

CHAPTER 11

Madison Swift sat across from me in the sheriff's office, her hands trembling as she struggled with a confession that had nothing to do with murder and everything to do with hearts making choices that defied logic.

"I wasn't alone the night Dakota died," she said finally, her words barely audible. "I was with someone. Someone who's married."

Emmet leaned forward, recognizing the significance of Madison's admission. "We'll need to verify that alibi, Madison. A murder investigation takes precedence over personal privacy."

"I know," Madison replied, tears gathering in her eyes. "That's why I've been trying to find another way to prove my innocence. I didn't want to destroy a family just to save myself."

The moral complexity of Madison's situation was evident in her anguished expression. She'd been willing to face murder charges rather than expose an affair that would devastate innocent people, demonstrating integrity that made her guilt increasingly unlikely.

"His wife doesn't know," Madison continued, her voice breaking under the weight of secrets that had become unbearable. "They have kids. A whole life together. But the pressure of this investigation made me realize I couldn't let myself be wrongly convicted when I have an alibi that could clear me."

"Who was with you?" I asked gently, recognizing that Madison's emotional state required careful handling despite the urgency of our investigation.

"Tom Bradley," Madison whispered, naming one of the van life community's more established members. "He's been struggling with marriage problems for months. We connected over shared interests, and it just... happened. One night turned into something neither of us expected."

Emmet consulted his notes about community members, finding Tom Bradley listed among the families camping at the meadow during Dakota's murder. "He was there with his wife and two children?"

"Yes," Madison confirmed, fresh tears flowing as she contemplated the destruction her confession might cause. "They've been trying to work through problems, and an affair revelation could end everything for them. But I can't let innocent people be arrested for something they didn't do."

Within an hour, Emmet had discreetly contacted

Tom Bradley and requested a private conversation away from his family campsite. The man's face went ashen when he realized his secret was about to be exposed, but his relief at clearing Madison was evident despite his personal devastation.

"Madison was with me from 11:00 p.m. until around four in the morning," Tom confirmed, his voice heavy with shame and exhaustion. "We've been meeting whenever our camping locations overlapped. I know it's wrong, but my marriage has been... difficult."

The timeline completely cleared Madison of involvement in Dakota's murder, which had occurred between midnight and 3:00 a.m. according to forensic estimates. Tom's confirmation, combined with the emotional authenticity of their confessions, provided unshakeable alibi verification.

"We'll need written statements from both of you," Emmet said, balancing investigation necessities with compassion for the personal destruction these revelations would cause. "The information will remain confidential unless required for court proceedings."

Madison's clearance left Jake Morrison as our final suspect among the obvious candidates, but his medical situation presented complications that required careful investigation. His claims of food poisoning and fever-induced confusion needed verification through official medical records rather than simple acceptance of his word.

"When we contacted Jake for follow-up questions about his alibi, he mentioned that his memories of that night are fuzzy due to high fever," I told Emmet as we drove toward the urgent care clinic where Jake claimed to have received treatment. "If that's true, it explains why he couldn't provide a clear alibi initially."

"And if it's false, it's a convenient excuse for inconsistent statements," Emmet replied, though his tone suggested growing doubt about Jake's guilt. "Medical records don't lie, so we'll know within the hour."

The urgent care clinic's records department confirmed that Jake Morrison had indeed been treated for severe food poisoning during the exact timeframe of Dakota's murder. The attending physician remembered the case clearly due to Jake's extremely high fever and the consideration given to hospitalization.

"Patient was delirious and disoriented due to fever of 104.2 degrees," the doctor explained while reviewing Jake's file. "We kept him under observation from midnight until 5:00 a.m. because of dehydration concerns and temperature instability."

The medical documentation was comprehensive and unforgiving. Jake's vital signs had been monitored hourly, medications administered on schedule, and nursing notes detailed his condition throughout the night. Multiple staff members had interacted with him during the crucial timeframe, providing witnesses beyond simple paper records.

"His fever was high enough to affect memory formation," the physician continued, explaining Jake's genuine confusion about the timeline. "Patients often have gaps or false memories from periods of extreme hyperthermia. His inability to recall details clearly was a direct result of his medical condition."

Jake's clearance through objective medical evidence left us with an investigation that had systematically eliminated every obvious suspect while the real killer remained hidden among those we'd considered helpful and trustworthy. Frank Brennan, Madison Swift, and Jake Morrison had all provided compelling reasons for suspicion, but none had actually committed murder.

"We're back to Sarah Beth," I said as we returned to the sheriff's office. "Everyone else has been cleared through verifiable evidence."

"But we need more than suspicious behavior and fraudulent business practices to prove murder," Emmet replied, recognizing the gap between knowing Sarah Beth's guilt and proving it in court. "We need direct evidence placing her at the crime scene or witness testimony about her activities that night."

The investigation had reached a crucial juncture where circumstantial evidence pointed clearly toward Sarah Beth's guilt, but prosecution required concrete proof that would survive legal challenges. Her counterfeit equipment scheme provided motive, her technical knowledge supplied means, but establishing opportunity demanded witness testimony or physical evidence we hadn't yet discovered.

"Someone must have seen her that night," I said, reviewing the timeline of events around Dakota's murder. "She couldn't have approached the crime scene without being noticed by someone in the van life community."

Before Emmet could respond, his office phone rang. The caller identification showed a local number, but the voice was unfamiliar and shaking with obvious emotional distress.

"This is Helen Coleman," the caller said, her words barely audible through tears and what sounded like barely controlled panic. "I'm Sarah Beth's mother. I need to speak with someone about my daughter and that young person's death."

The timing of Helen Coleman's call felt significant beyond coincidence, arriving precisely when our investigation needed definitive evidence to connect Sarah Beth to Dakota's murder. But the emotional weight in her voice suggested this wasn't calculated timing, but rather the breaking point of someone who'd been wrestling with terrible knowledge.

"Mrs. Coleman, this is Sheriff Quill," Emmet replied, activating the speaker function so I could participate in the conversation. "What information do you have about Dakota Rivers' death?"

"I found my daughter's diary," Helen said, her voice breaking with the pain of betraying family loyalty for the sake of justice. "She left it open on her kitchen table when I stopped by to bring her dinner three days ago. I saw what she wrote about that night, about what she did to that poor young person."

The revelation sent electricity through the sheriff's office. Sarah Beth's own mother had discovered written evidence of her daughter's guilt, providing the definitive proof our investigation required.

"What did the diary say?" I asked gently, recognizing the emotional complexity of a mother's position when discovering her child had committed murder.

"She wrote about sabotaging that climbing harness before selling it to Dakota," Helen explained, her voice growing stronger as she committed to full disclosure. "She knew Dakota was investigating her business practices and planned to expose the counterfeit equipment operation. The diary entry describes exactly how she weakened the gear so it would fail under stress."

The confession provided comprehensive evidence of premeditation and method, transforming our circumstantial case into concrete proof of deliberate murder. Sarah Beth had documented her own criminal planning in writing, creating evidence that would be devastating in court proceedings.

"Why didn't you come forward immediately after finding this?" Emmet asked, balancing gentle questioning with the need for details about the timeline.

"Because she's my daughter," Helen replied simply, her words carrying the weight of maternal love struggling against moral obligation. "I've been trying to process what I read, hoping there was some other explanation. But watching innocent people being investigated while I know the truth... I can't let that continue."

"Mrs. Coleman, we'll need you to come in and provide a formal statement," Emmet said, recognizing the crucial importance of preserving this testimony through proper legal procedures. "Your information could be vital to solving this case."

"I know what this means for Sarah Beth," Helen

replied, her voice heavy with the knowledge that her testimony would likely result in her daughter's arrest for murder. "But I can't let innocent people suffer for what she's done. That's not how I raised her."

After scheduling Helen Coleman's formal interview, Emmet and I sat in contemplative silence as we processed the implications of her testimony. Combined with the evidence of Sarah Beth's counterfeit equipment scheme and her suspicious knowledge of crime scene details, her mother's witness account provided the final piece needed for criminal prosecution.

"We have motive through the equipment fraud scheme, means through her technical knowledge, and now opportunity through her mother's testimony," Emmet said, organizing the evidence that had accumulated against Sarah Beth. "Plus, her behavior throughout the investigation has been consistently deceptive and manipulative."

"She's been playing helpful business owner while monitoring our progress and deflecting suspicion toward obvious red herrings," I added. "Every piece of assistance she offered was designed to keep herself above suspicion while guiding us toward convenient suspects."

The pattern was undeniable in retrospect. Sarah Beth had positioned herself as an essential resource for the investigation while systematically misdirecting our attention toward Frank Brennan's financial desperation, Madison Swift's professional rivalry, and Jake Morrison's obsessive stalking. Her helpfulness had been a carefully constructed facade designed to hide her guilt while ensuring other people faced suspicion for her crime.

"Frank, Madison, and Jake were perfect red herrings because they all had compelling motives and suspicious behavior," I observed, recognizing how Sarah Beth had exploited obvious suspects to protect herself. "But none of them actually committed murder."

"While Sarah Beth remained invisible among the helpful community members we trusted most," Emmet concluded, understanding how the real killer had hidden in plain sight throughout our entire investigation.

Helen Coleman's courageous decision to prioritize justice over family loyalty had provided the breakthrough our investigation required, but it came at enormous personal cost. Her testimony would likely result in her daughter's arrest and conviction for murder, destroying their family relationship while exposing a criminal enterprise that had put countless lives at risk.

The van life community would finally have answers about Dakota Rivers' murder, but the resolution would reveal that their safety had been systematically compromised by someone they'd trusted to provide reliable equipment for their adventures. Sarah Beth Coleman had turned outdoor recreation into Russian roulette, selling death disguised as safety while collecting profits from both the initial fraud and subsequent cover-up activities.

Our investigation had come full circle from obvious suspects to the truth hidden among those we'd considered above suspicion. Sarah Beth's helpful facade had concealed a criminal mind capable of murder to protect a fraudulent empire built on counterfeit equipment and customer endangerment.

CHAPTER 12

The brass bells chimed cheerfully as we entered Rustic Trails Outfitters, their innocent melody contrasting sharply with the knowledge that we were confronting a killer. Sarah Beth looked up from her inventory sheets with the helpful smile of a business owner greeting valued customers.

"Sheriff Quill, Sage! What a pleasant surprise," she said, her voice carrying the cooperative tone that had concealed her guilt throughout our investigation. "I hope you're here with good news about solving poor Dakota's murder. The whole community has been so concerned about safety."

"Actually, we have some follow-up questions about the manufacturer information you provided," Emmet said, maintaining the routine tone that suggested continued cooperation rather than suspicion. "The warranty department has been very helpful with their investigation."

Sarah Beth's eyes brightened with what appeared to be genuine interest. "Wonderful! I'm so glad my contacts proved useful. Have they identified any patterns in the equipment failures? I've been worried that there might be a broader safety issue affecting multiple retailers."

Her concerned act was flawless, demonstrating the calculated performance that had kept her above suspicion while we investigated obvious red herrings. I detected smugness beneath her helpful demeanor as she believed she was successfully manipulating our investigation.

"Actually, they discovered some very interesting patterns," I said, watching Sarah Beth's emotional signature for any flicker of concern. "Patterns that go beyond simple manufacturing defects."

"Oh?" Sarah Beth replied, tilting her head with curiosity that seemed completely authentic. "What kind of patterns?"

"Fraudulent warranty claims," Emmet said bluntly, watching Sarah Beth's face for reaction. "Claims for equipment that manufacturers never actually sold to retailers."

The change in Sarah Beth's expression was subtle but unmistakable. Her helpful smile faltered for just a moment before reasserting itself, but my magical perception caught the spike of alarm beneath her controlled façade.

"That sounds terrible," she said, her voice maintaining its concerned tone despite the underlying tension I could detect. "Identity theft affecting businesses? How awful for legitimate retailers who might be blamed for criminal activity they had nothing to do with."

"The thing is, Sarah Beth," Emmet continued, his tone shifting from conversational to official, "the fraudulent claims all trace back to this store. Your store."

Sarah Beth's confident mask cracked enough to reveal genuine panic before she managed to reassert control. "That's impossible. I keep meticulous records of all my purchases and warranty claims. There must be some mistake in their database."

"No mistake," I said quietly, reading the fear now radiating from Sarah Beth like heat from a fire. "We know about the counterfeit equipment operation. We know about Dakota's investigation that threatened to expose you. And we know you killed them to protect your criminal enterprise."

"I have no idea what you're talking about," Sarah Beth replied, but her voice carried a tremor that betrayed her growing panic. "I run a legitimate business serving the outdoor recreation community. These accusations are completely unfounded."

"Your mother found your diary, Sarah Beth," Emmet said with quiet authority. "She read your confession about sabotaging Dakota's climbing harness. She knows what you did, and she couldn't live with innocent people being suspected for your crime."

The revelation hit Sarah Beth like a sledgehammer. Her carefully maintained composure shattered completely as she realized her written documentation of the murder had been discovered. Her face went ashen, her hands began shaking, and my senses detected the complete collapse of her emotional control.

"My mother..." Sarah Beth whispered, the betrayal evident in her voice. "She read my private diary?"

"She found it open on your kitchen table," I explained, watching Sarah Beth process the catastrophic failure of her security. "Open to the page where you described exactly how you weakened Dakota's climbing harness so it would fail under stress."

Sarah Beth's legs seemed to give out beneath her. She grabbed the edge of her sales counter for support, her breathing becoming rapid and shallow as panic overwhelmed her calculated planning.

"It was creative writing," she said desperately, grasping for any explanation that might save her. "Fiction. A story I was working on about a murder mystery. None of it was real."

"Your diary entry included specific technical details about the sabotage method that match exactly how Dakota's harness failed," Emmet replied, his voice carrying the certainty of someone presenting irrefutable evidence. "Details that only the killer would know."

Sarah Beth's desperate denials crumbled as she realized the futility of continuing her lies. Her shoulders sagged with defeat, and when she looked up at us again, her helpful front had been replaced by exhausted resignation.

"You don't understand the pressure I was under," she said, her voice breaking as years of careful deception finally collapsed. "My business was failing. The counterfeit equipment was the only thing keeping me afloat financially."

"So you murdered Dakota to protect your illegal profits?" I asked, detecting the mixture of guilt and self-righteousness that had driven Sarah Beth to kill.

"Dakota was going to destroy everything!" Sarah Beth exploded, her composure completely shattered as months of suppressed fear and anger poured out. "Their exposé would have revealed the counterfeit operation, led to criminal charges, destroyed my reputation. I would have lost my business, my home, everything I'd worked for."

"So you decided to eliminate the threat," Emmet said, recognizing the calculated nature of Sarah Beth's crime.

"I tried to convince myself there was another way,"

Sarah Beth continued, her confession tumbling out in a torrent of justification and desperation. "But Dakota wouldn't listen to reason. They were obsessed with their investigation, determined to expose what they called 'systematic safety violations.' They didn't care about the collateral damage their exposé would cause."

"Collateral damage?" I asked, horrified by Sarah Beth's characterization of her criminal enterprise as legitimate business.

"I employed three people! I supported local outdoor recreation! I provided affordable equipment to van lifers who couldn't afford premium gear!" Sarah Beth's voice rose with self-righteous anger. "Dakota was going to destroy all of that for the sake of viral content and subscriber growth."

Her justification revealed the twisted logic that had allowed her to commit murder while maintaining belief in her own righteousness. In Sarah Beth's mind, she was protecting her community from an exploitative content creator, not eliminating a threat to her criminal activities.

"So you sabotaged their climbing harness," Emmet said, keeping Sarah Beth focused on her confession.

"I knew their equipment preferences from previous purchases," Sarah Beth admitted, her voice hollow with exhausted defeat. "I weakened the webbing at specific stress points, then called them about a 'special deal' on professional-grade gear for their content creation. They came in excited about getting premium equipment at a discount."

The cold calculation behind Dakota's murder was staggering. Sarah Beth had exploited Dakota's enthusiasm for authentic content to sell them the weapon that would kill them, disguising murder as customer service.

"You watched them die," I said, detecting the complex emotions surrounding Sarah Beth's memories of that night.

"I didn't watch," Sarah Beth protested, though her emotional signature suggested otherwise. "I gave them the equipment and left. I thought... I hoped it would look like a manufacturing defect when it failed."

"But you knew it would fail," Emmet pressed, establishing the premeditation that would be crucial for prosecution.

"I calculated the stress tolerances precisely," Sarah Beth admitted, her technical knowledge revealing itself in her confession. "The harness would support static weight but fail under dynamic loading. It was designed to look like an equipment malfunction rather than sabotage."

"Until our investigation revealed the deliberate

nature of the failure," I observed, recognizing how Sarah Beth's careful planning had unraveled under forensic examination.

"I never expected such thorough analysis," Sarah Beth said, her voice carrying bitter regret at her tactical miscalculation. "Most equipment failures are written off as user error or manufacturing defects. I thought the investigation would be superficial."

"You thought wrong," Emmet replied grimly. "And now you're under arrest for the murder of Dakota Rivers."

But Sarah Beth wasn't finished. Her confession had revealed the scope of her criminal enterprise, but her eyes were darting toward the back office where she kept documentation of her counterfeit supplier network and fraudulent warranty claims.

"I need to get something from my office," she said, moving toward the door behind her sales counter with sudden urgency. "Important business records that need to be secured."

I felt her desperate calculation rather than legitimate business concern. Sarah Beth was planning something that had nothing to do with securing records and everything to do with destroying evidence.

"Sarah Beth, stop," Emmet commanded, but she was already through the office door.

I heard the sound of furniture being overturned and papers rustling frantically before catching the distinctive smell of kerosene. My witch senses screamed danger as I realized Sarah Beth's intention.

"She's trying to burn the evidence!" I shouted, rushing toward the office door.

Through the office window, I could see Sarah Beth holding a lit kerosene lamp above stacks of papers and file cabinets. Her face was illuminated by the flame, twisted with desperate determination to destroy the documentation that would prove her criminal enterprise.

"If I can't have my business, no one can have the evidence!" she screamed, preparing to smash the lamp onto the pile of papers that represented years of criminal activity.

My magical awareness allowed me to anticipate her movement a split second before she acted. I tackled Sarah Beth just as she raised the lamp, sending both of us crashing into the file cabinets as the kerosene lamp shattered against the wall, spreading flaming fuel across the floor.

"Emmet!" I called out, struggling to restrain Sarah Beth while flames spread rapidly through the office. "Fire extinguisher!"

Emmet burst through the door with a commercial fire extinguisher from the store's front area, quickly suppressing the flames before they could consume the crucial documentation. Sarah Beth fought desperately in my grip, trying to reach the remaining papers even as smoke filled the small office space.

"It's over, Sarah Beth," I said, using my full strength to pin her arms behind her back while Emmet finished extinguishing the fire. "The evidence is preserved, your confession is recorded, and you're under arrest for murder."

Sarah Beth's resistance finally collapsed as she realized that even her desperate arson attempt had failed. Her criminal enterprise was exposed, her mother had betrayed her trust, and the evidence that would convict her remained intact despite her efforts at destruction.

"I just wanted to build something," she whispered, tears streaming down her face. "I wanted to be successful, to matter in this community. I never meant for things to go so far."

"You sold counterfeit equipment that could have killed dozens of people," Emmet said as he secured handcuffs around Sarah Beth's wrists. "Dakota Rivers was just the first person to die from your criminal negligence."

"River Martinez nearly died from sabotaged gear you sold him after Dakota's murder," I added, ensuring Sarah Beth understood the full scope of her crimes. "You continued selling dangerous equipment even during the investigation."

Sarah Beth had no response to the litany of her crimes. Her helpful business owner mask had been completely stripped away, revealing the criminal mind that had treated customer safety as expendable in pursuit of illegal profits.

As backup deputies arrived to secure the scene and catalog evidence, I reflected on how Sarah Beth had hidden among the people we'd trusted most. Her helpful cooperation had been calculated manipulation designed to deflect suspicion while we chased obvious red herrings.

Frank Brennan's financial desperation, Madison Swift's professional rivalry, and Jake Morrison's obsessive stalking had all provided compelling motives for murder, but none had actually killed Dakota Rivers. The real killer had been selling them safety equipment while planning their death, concealing murder behind customer service and community support.

"The van life community can finally feel safe," Emmet said as Sarah Beth was loaded into a patrol car for transport to jail. "No more counterfeit equipment, no more fraudulent business practices, and justice for Dakota's murder."

The investigation had come full circle from obvious suspects to the truth hidden among those we'd considered above suspicion. Sarah Beth Coleman's criminal enterprise was exposed, her victims would receive justice, and the outdoor recreation community would be protected from her dangerous counterfeit equipment scheme.

Dakota Rivers had died trying to protect other van lifers from exactly the kind of criminal negligence that Sarah Beth represented. Their investigation would now be completed by law enforcement, ensuring that Sarah Beth's conviction would serve as warning to other businesses that put profits above customer safety.

The helpful store owner who'd guided our investigation toward innocent suspects while concealing her own guilt was finally facing consequences for her crimes. Rustic Trails Outfitters would be closed permanently, its inventory seized as evidence, and its owner imprisoned for murder and systematic fraud.

The meadow could return to being a peaceful gathering place for van lifers seeking authentic outdoor experiences, free from the threat of equipment sabotaged by someone they'd trusted to keep them safe. Sarah Beth Coleman's reign of criminal negligence was over, and her victim could finally rest in peace knowing their killer had been exposed and punished.

CHAPTER 13

Three weeks after we'd arrested Sarah Beth Coleman for murder, Emmet suggested we return to the meadow for another picnic. I had to admire his optimism. Our last romantic attempt at this exact location had ended with counterfeit climbing gear, attempted arson, and me tackling a killer in a smoke-filled office. But sure, let's give outdoor dining another shot.

"You realize this place has a terrible track record for our relationship," I pointed out while packing the same wicker basket Aunt Hecate had forced on us weeks ago. The universe apparently had a sense of humor about recycling props for our romantic disasters.

"That's exactly why we need to reclaim it," Emmet replied, though his energy was buzzing with something that felt distinctly un-picnic-like. My witch instincts were picking up nervous excitement mixed with what could charitably be called terror. Either he was planning something big, or he'd developed a sudden phobia of outdoor food.

The drive felt different this time. No emergency calls crackling over the radio, no urgent investigations pulling us toward crime scenes. Just two people heading toward what should theoretically be a normal evening. Of course, normal wasn't exactly my specialty, but I was willing to pretend.

When we crested the hill overlooking the meadow, I had to admit the van life community had outdone themselves. Twinkling lights stretched between trees like captured fireflies, and soft acoustic music drifted across the evening air with suspicious perfection.

"Someone's been busy," I observed, though my supernatural radar was pinging with something that felt oddly orchestrated. "It's like they're expecting something."

"Maybe they're just celebrating feeling safe again," Emmet said with the kind of forced casualness that immediately made me suspicious.

We found our spot near the oak tree where Dakota had died. It should have felt morbid, but instead it felt like honoring their memory... choosing love over fear, life over death. Emmet spread our blanket.

"This is nice," I said, settling onto the blanket and automatically extending my magical awareness across the meadow. That's when I noticed something deeply weird. "Emmet. Where the heck is everyone?"

I could sense the van lifers throughout the campground, their emotional signatures scattered like warm beacons in my supernatural perception, but they were all maintaining a remarkably strategic distance from our little corner of romance. Van lifers were social creatures by nature. They didn't just avoid people without reason.

"Privacy?" Emmet suggested weakly, fumbling with a wine bottle like his hands had forgotten how basic motor functions worked. "People respect romantic dinners."

"Since when do you know anything about van life etiquette?" I asked, accepting wine while my witch senses screamed that something was about to happen. "And why are you vibrating with more nervous energy than you had during Sarah Beth's arrest?"

"I'm not nervous," he protested, immediately knocking over the wine bottle. "I'm relaxed. Enjoying a peaceful evening with my girlfriend."

The music from the distant campsites was perfect... too perfect. Like someone had curated a playlist specifically designed for maximum emotional impact. My magical instincts were practically doing backflips trying to get my attention.

"Emmet," I said slowly, pieces clicking into place with supernatural clarity, "what are you planning?"

His attempt at innocence would have been adorable if it wasn't so transparent. "Nothing. Just a picnic."

"The van lifers are hiding like they're watching a show. There's romantic music coming from strategically placed speakers across the entire meadow. And you're acting like you're about to either propose or confess to embezzling county funds."

Emmet's face went through several expressions before settling on sheepish resignation. "I had a whole speech planned," he admitted, reaching into his jacket. "About how much you mean to me and wanting to spend the rest of my life solving supernatural mysteries with you."

My heart performed some kind of acrobatic maneuver that should have been physically impossible. Even my enhanced magical constitution couldn't regulate the sudden cardiac chaos.

"But then I realized speeches aren't really us," he continued, pulling out a small velvet box that practically hummed with possibility. "We're more the couple that improvises, adapts to magical chaos, and somehow makes it work despite the universe's apparent commitment to complicating our romantic moments."

The ring inside was perfect. It was elegant without being flashy, classic without being boring. Exactly what I would have chosen if I'd been brave enough to imagine this moment actually happening.

"Sage Poe," Emmet said, his voice steady now that he'd committed to the moment, "will you marry me? Will you keep figuring out this insane life with me, investigating supernatural crimes and having picnic dinners that get derailed by murder?"

I stared at the ring, then at Emmet's hopeful face, then at the meadow where an entire van life community was undoubtedly holding its collective breath behind various vehicles.

"You orchestrated this whole thing," I said as understanding dawned. "The lights, the music, the strategic van lifer exodus. You turned our former crime scene into a proposal venue."

"River and Willow were surprisingly enthusiastic about the planning," Emmet admitted. "Turns out van lifers take romance very seriously."

"How long have you been carrying that ring around?" I asked, realizing he'd had it during Sarah Beth's arrest, the store confrontation, all the dramatic final moments of our investigation.

"I figured if we could survive catching a killer

together, marriage would be manageable," he said with the kind of pragmatic romanticism that made him perfect for someone whose life involved regular supernatural mayhem. "Plus, I wanted to propose somewhere meaningful to us, even if that somewhere happened to be a former crime scene. It seemed like the kind of thing you'd appreciate."

Tears were gathering in my eyes, which was ridiculous because I wasn't a crying person. But something about Emmet's faith in our future, his willingness to build something beautiful in a place that had seen so much darkness, hit me right in the emotional center I usually kept carefully armored.

"Yes," I said, the word escaping before my brain caught up. "Obviously, yes."

Emmet's grin could have powered the entire state as he slipped the ring onto my finger. It fit perfectly, which meant either excellent detective work or some kind of supernatural intervention in the jewelry department.

"I love you, Sage," he said, pulling me into a kiss that tasted like wine and possibilities.

"I love you too," I replied, my mind confirming what my heart already knew. This was exactly right, exactly what was supposed to happen.

From across the meadow came applause and cheering as the van life community emerged from their hiding spots like the world's most enthusiastic flash mob. River and Willow led the charge, followed by Tank Williams and several other people who'd apparently invested significant emotional energy in the success of Emmet's proposal.

"We've been planning this for two weeks!" Willow announced, tears streaming down her weathered cheeks. "Van lifers are excellent at complex logistical operations."

"The lights were Tank's contribution," Emmet explained as champagne appeared from someone's seemingly endless outdoor gear collection. "Military pedantry applied to romantic ambiance."

"Seemed appropriate," Tank said. "Good operational symmetry."

As the community gathered around us to celebrate, I realized Emmet had done something remarkable. He'd transformed a place associated with death and deception into the setting for a celebration of life and love. It was either deeply poetic or slightly twisted, depending on your perspective. I liked it either way.

"Did someone say engagement party?" called a familiar voice, and I turned to see Angelica, Lovage, and Aunt Hecate emerging from behind River's Airstream like they'd been hiding there all along.

"You were in on this too?" I asked, though I was laughing too hard to sound accusatory.

"Honey, Emmet asked for our blessing two weeks ago," Aunt Hecate said, her eyes twinkling with mischief despite the binding marks that still shadowed her features. "Did you think he'd propose without consulting your family first?"

"I helped pick the ring," Angelica added with obvious pride. "My enhanced perception is excellent for evaluating diamond quality."

"And I researched optimal proposal timing based on lunar cycles and supernatural energy patterns," Lovage contributed, pulling out a tablet covered in charts and calculations. "Tonight was statistically the most romantically auspicious evening for the next six months."

"You people are ridiculous," I said, but my magical awareness was practically singing with the love and support radiating from my chosen family. Both my blood relatives and van life adoptees.

"No more murder investigations during romantic dinners," I declared, raising my champagne as stars began appearing overhead.

"I'll do my best," Emmet replied, "but considering your family's supernatural tendencies and my job as sheriff, I'm not promising completely normal romantic experiences."

"Good," I said, clinking my glass against his while

our unconventional chosen family cheered around us. "Normal is overrated anyway."

The meadow settled into peaceful celebration as the evening deepened. Music played from hidden speakers, lights twinkled like earthbound stars, and the van life community that had adopted us shared stories and laughter that carried across the water.

For once, there were no supernatural threats lurking in the shadows, no murders demanding investigation, no criminal enterprises requiring exposure. Just two people who'd found each other despite the chaos, surrounded by friends and family who'd helped them celebrate whatever came next.

"Mrs. Quill," Emmet said experimentally.

"Sage Poe-Quill," I corrected, because I wasn't abandoning my family name or my identity as a witch just because I was getting married. "Partnership, not absorption."

"Sage Poe-Quill," he agreed, and somehow he made it sound like the most beautiful name in the world.

The meadow stretched around us like a promise of all the adventures we'd share, all the mysteries we'd solve together, and all the romantic dinners that might or might not get interrupted by supernatural emergencies. I couldn't wait to find out what came next.

The diamond on my finger caught the firelight and scattered sparkles across our faces, and for the first time in a long time, the future felt less like something to survive and more like something to celebrate.

Thank you for reading!

© Sara Bourgeois 2025

This story is a work of fiction. Any resemblance to persons alive or dead is a coincidence.

Made in United States
Troutdale, OR
07/06/2025